LOVE ME FOREVER

CAREY JANE CLARK

Hope Springs Press

Please note that this book is also offered free as a special VIP Club subscriber reward:

To receive your free copy, please visit careyjaneclark.com

Carey Jane Clark's VIP Club members receive freebies, behind-the-scenes information, and unique items to accompany her books.

Members are always the first to hear about Carey's new books and publications.

1

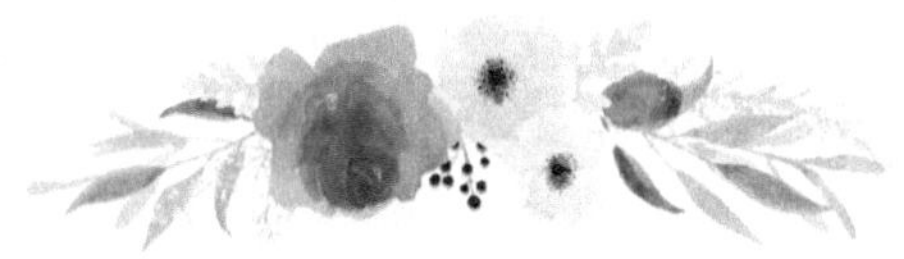

The breeze off the lake held the scent of sun and summer—and hope. I stood outside the back door of the cottage on the cracked patio slab and stared at the shimmering waters of Lake Ontario. My seven-year-old grandson Caleb laughed and ran in the waves with Hershey, his chocolate lab. I briefly wished for my camera. The scene would make a beautiful painting. But I had somewhere to be.

Celia sat watching from a blanket on the beach. She shielded her eyes from the August sun as I walked toward the shore.

"You're going out?" she called.

I walked a few more steps before replying, knowing how one's voice could be carried away by the wind and rolling waves.

"Just headed into town to take care of an errand."

Celia glanced out at the lake. Caleb lay on his back in the shallow water, and Hershey stood over him, barking and nudging him to play. "Do you want us to go with you? Caleb cleans up pretty fast."

I waved a hand at her. "Don't be silly. He's having way too much fun out there."

"Everything okay, Mom?" Celia looked me over. "I mean— don't get me wrong. That's a beautiful suit but—"

"Everything's just fine, honey. Like I said, just a little errand I need to run." I waved at Caleb, who waved back. "I should be home in plenty of time for lunch, but just in case, there is pasta salad in the fridge, and if Caleb gets the munchies—"

"We'll be fine, Mom, really. I'm sure I can find my way around the cottage kitchen." She was right, of course. She'd been coming here every summer since she was younger than Caleb was now.

"Okay, well I won't be long. Have fun." I picked through the sand in my heels, across the back yard and up the hill to the gravel drive. Before I hopped in the car, I checked the mailbox and pulled out the package of letters and flyers and plopped them on the passenger seat of my Volkswagen Jetta. I put the car in reverse, and backed out the driveway, trying to calm my nerves. I didn't keep many secrets from my daughter, but I felt the need to keep quiet about this—at least until later in the day. Celia was a model daughter, but far too practical for her own good sometimes. This was something I didn't want to be talked out of.

I drove into town and parked in front of the store three doors from the corner of Main and Queen Streets. In spite of the flutter of butterflies that seemed to have taken residence in my stomach, I smiled. I envisioned planters lining the wide windows and the sign overhead with the business name I'd already registered: Every Bloomin' Thing.

A knock on my car window roused me from my daydream. Jo-Ann Simpson waved. "Today's the day," she said as I stepped out of the car.

I followed her to the front door. She ushered me in, and I was surrounded by the familiar scent of fresh flowers and dried eucalyptus. She handed me a set of keys. "These are yours now. The smaller one is for the delivery entrance." She motioned toward the back room—the one that would double as a space to prepare bouquets and flower arrangements. And my new art studio. "Come on and we'll get your signature on all this paperwork."

I took a deep breath. This was really happening. It was only the first step of many of course. I'd have to list the house in Point-du-Fleuve, pack up my things and move them into the smaller summer house, but I'd already quit my job and taken steps to winterize the cottage. And my friend Jack, a retired investment lawyer, had been over all the paperwork and my business plan with me and given his stamp of approval. "That'll give you a solid start," he'd said. "And I applaud your effort to develop two streams of income. You sure you can do that right out of the gate, though? Run the flower shop *and* the painting studio?"

But I'd never been more sure of anything in my life. This shop was the fruition of ten years of dreaming and five years of planning. I'd pushed art out of my life for a long time—for practically all of Celia's growing-up years. But I'd been working away at it in the spare room of the house ever since she married and moved to Toronto with Jeff. When they moved back to Point-du-Fleuve and started a family, I still dabbled when I wasn't doing grandma duty. And for the last five years, I'd allowed myself to start thinking about turning it all into something more. I planned to hang a few select paintings for sale in the retail space. The rest of the storefront would remain a florist shop. I'd maintain and grow the business I was taking over and run evening art classes in the studio in back. It's a model I'd seen work elsewhere, and I knew I was the one to make it work in the newly-trendy little town of Port Sandford.

When I heard that Jo-Ann planned to retire and was looking for someone to take over the business she'd built over the last thirty years, I knew this was just the opportunity I'd been waiting for. Jo-Ann knew it too. We'd known each other to pass on the street, but we bonded over that first conversation about her business. She took my hand across the table.

"Adele, this shop is my baby," she said. "It's hard to walk away from your baby and leave it in the hands of a stranger. But I feel so good know ing you'll be the one taking things over. And I love your ideas for the art studio. I think that's just the direction that will breathe new life into things. In fact, I'd love to be one of your first students."

My pen hovered over the signature line, I glanced at Jo-Ann with a nervous giggle, then took a deep breath and signed my name. That simple act felt ground-breaking—the biggest change my life had seen in thirty years.

But then I didn't know what waited for me later that day.

I drove back to the cottage in a daze, barely able to believe I'd actually done it. I was a business owner.

I pulled onto Pinetree Lane, the small road that wound down from the main road to the few cottages that bordered the lake, among which mine was nestled. I stopped the car and hopped out when I rounded the curve and came upon my long-time neighbor and good friend Jack Murphy strolling along the lane with his dog, Pepper.

"I did it," I announced.

Jack laughed. "Well, hello to you too!"

I laughed with him. "Hi, Jack. I've just come back from town. I signed all the paperwork. It's official. I'm now owner of Jo-Ann's Flower Shop, soon to be renamed Every Bloomin' Thing."

"Congratulations." Jack hugged me, leaving me with a

lingering hint of the spicy aroma of his cologne. "How does it feel?"

"Wonderful." I released the breath it seemed I'd been holding since I left town. "And scary. Really scary. But mostly wonderful."

"You'll do great." Jack exuded the confidence I'd come to know him for. He and his late wife Emma had built their lavish cottage here around the time Celia graduated from high school —just as our humble little laneway became a real estate agent's dream: prime cottage area along the lakefront in a market of people hungry for a quiet retreat from the noise and traffic of Toronto, seventy-five miles away.

Jack stepped closer and took my hand. "We should celebrate. How about tonight I take you out to that new restaurant in town."

I blushed, unused to this kind of attention from him. "That one with the fancy menu items with names bigger than their serving sizes?"

Jack grinned. "That's just the one. The occasion demands ostentation, don't you think? We'll order their most expensive bottle of champagne to toast your success."

I glanced toward the lake. Even from here I could hear Caleb's squeals of laughter as he and Hershey played who-knows-what kind of raucous game along the shore. "My daughter and grandson are here for the week."

"Oh." Jack's shoulders slumped a little. But he recovered quickly. "On the weekend, then?"

I smiled. "Sounds wonderful."

Jack looked down at my hand, which he still held in his, then his eyes met mine again. "I'll hold you to it. I'm not going to let such a special occasion go unmarked."

I felt the flush in my cheeks again. "Okay. It's-it's a date, then."

We said our good-byes and I hopped back in the car and

drove the few remaining yards to my driveway and pulled in. I grabbed my purse and the bundle of mail from the passenger seat and dashed to the cottage. I swung open the door, prepared to tell Celia and Caleb my exciting news, but met Caleb on the mat. He'd just come in, dripping wet.

"Caleb, you're making a puddle on the floor," Celia flew at him with a towel.

I laughed. "Don't worry about it, honey. This floor has seen plenty of wet bodies. Don't you remember how you and Sarah used to come in from the lake dripping wet? Wetter than that, I dare say."

Celia grinned. "You're exaggerating, Mom. I'm sure we were never quite *this* wet."

I reached for plates to serve the pasta salad. "How is Sarah, anyway? I haven't heard much about her for a while."

Celia continued scrubbing at Caleb with a beach towel. "She's good. She and Justin just came over the other day. She's had Justin in a lot of camps this summer. Dan's busy at the store and wanted her there with him. We offered to have him over at our place all summer. Caleb would have loved that. But Dan wouldn't have it." She gave Caleb's hair a final buffing with the towel. "Go get dressed for lunch."

"Aw, Mom. Do I have to?"

"Well, put a T-shirt on, at least." She patted his backside and sent him off to his room—her old room—in search of another layer.

The table set, I picked up the stack of mail I'd set on the kitchen counter and leafed through it. Some bills, a flyer or two, and one letter with familiar, distinctive handwriting. I tore it open and began to read.

Could it be?

"Dan and I don't really get along all the time, you know? Actually, I guess it's not so much that we don't get along as that we barely talk. He's a good guy, I guess. But I'd sure rather visit when he's not around. Let's just put it that way. It's a shame because I think he and Jeff would really hit it off if Dan would give him half a chance ... Mom, are you listening?"

"Mmmm ... Yes, I'm sorry. I was. I just ... there was a letter in the mail ..."

"Everything okay? You look pale." She stepped toward me and reached her hand toward the letter. "Let me see."

"No. No, that's okay. It's nothing. Just an old friend. I'll look at it later." I folded the letter closed and tucked it between the bills and flyers. I walked to the roll top desk in the corner, shoved the whole stack inside and closed the lid.

"Let's eat." I raised my voice. "Caleb, you ready yet?"

Celia's brow furrowed. Nevertheless, she turned and headed to Caleb's room, calling after him. I breathed a sigh of relief as I sat down and began to serve up the pasta salad. I didn't know what I would say if she demanded to know more about the letter. I had no idea how I would react to it myself—whether I would reply to it or throw it away or even if I'd finish reading it. I hadn't seen that handwriting for thirty years. I never thought I would again. I forced my thoughts to the present and smiled as Caleb careened out of the room and landed on the chair next to me.

Like I'd told Celia, I'd have to wait until later—when she wasn't around—to look at the letter from her father.

2

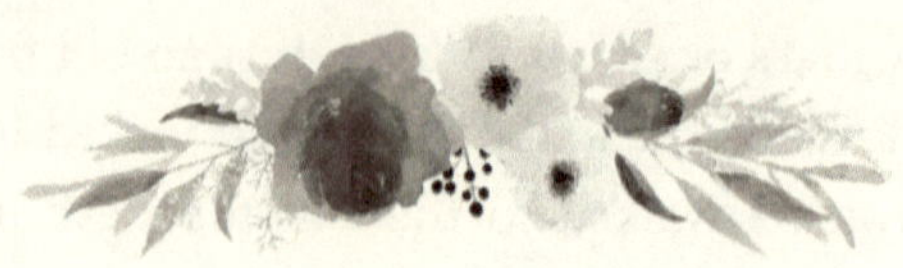

"I'd like to take you into town for lunch today." I kicked the sand with my bare feet. At Caleb's request, we'd come to hike the dunes. He ran ahead of us with Hershey, a towel draped over his shoulder, a stick in his hand.

"I'm a camel driver," he announced. As we crossed over the ridge headed away from the beach. the sandbanks of Prince Edward County did resemble a desert. A child's imagination furnished everything else needed to make that picture complete.

"Don't we have some leftovers in the fridge?"

I sighed. "Yes, we do, but that's not the point. You're leaving soon, and there's a little tea shop in town I'd like to take you to for lunch. Afterwards there's something in town I'd like to show you. And maybe we could take Caleb to the playground near the beach."

Celia scanned the sandbanks. Caleb had just disappeared over a rise and she quickened her pace. I laid a hand on her shoulder. "He'll be fine. Hershey's with him." Besides, I couldn't walk much faster through the sand and heat. I'd never catch up with a seven-year-old.

Celia grinned at me. "You're sounding kind of mysterious. What's this 'something in town' you want to show me?"

I patted her shoulder. "You'll just have to wait and see ..." My heart leaped a little. I didn't really know what Celia would think of my plans for the flower shop. She was always so practical, and this plan had a lot of dream in it. Her husband Jeff took a risk to begin working at home a few years back when they decided to move to Point-du-Fleuve. He'd taken advantage of a work-from-home program his firm in Toronto offered. With the right software and an internet connection, he'd been able to work as an architect from his office in their home.

But no one in our family had ever owned a business before. And now I did. Since signing the paperwork twenty-four hours ago that made me owner of the flower shop, I'd had to take plenty of deep breaths. It was still hard to believe, and I felt a constant unsteadiness in my stomach. Telling Celia today about my plans would be my first step in making it real. The plans weren't the only reason for my nerves, I knew. There was Jack's invitation to dinner. And I hadn't been able to stop thinking about that letter I'd stuffed in the roll top desk.

We reached the top of the dune and looked across them. "There he is." I pointed off to the right, where Caleb lay in the sand, Hershey beside him. Apparently, the camel or its driver needed a break.

When we caught up to him, Caleb looked up at me. "Is there still lemonade in the fridge, Gramma?"

"I think so, but if there isn't, we can make more."

"Okay. I'm hot. And thirsty."

I laughed. "Why don't we walk back along the beach so you can splash in the water a bit? And when we get back, we'll get ready to go into town."

He jumped up. "Can we go to the playground?"

Celia bent and picked up his towel. "After lunch. We'll eat first and then Gramma has something she wants to show us."

"Cool." Caleb knelt in the sand. "Did you hear that, Hershey? I get to go to the playground. Sorry. You'll have to stay back at Gramma's."

When we arrived back at the cottage, Celia pulled out the garden hose while Caleb stood on the patio slab outside the back door. She gave him a thorough hosing down. She stared at the long crack in the concrete that stretched from one end almost to the other and then broke off and spread in the other direction, making a "Y" across it. Grass grew in the cracks.

I didn't have to ask what she was thinking about. I only hoped she wouldn't say anything. We'd had that same conversation too many times. The patio slab had been a planned project of her father's before the divorce. He'd built the cottage and had planned to build an addition with a sunroom over this concrete slab. But it hadn't happened before he left, and perhaps it never would. Although maybe if the shop did well, I'd be able to find the resources to hire someone to do it. It would make a lovely spot to sit in the mornings before I went to work.

No child ever did especially well through a divorce, despite their parents' assurances to themselves that their kids were resilient. But Celia had taken it really hard when Alfie left. It was as though the sunshine had left her heart. And it marked the end of many things for her. We'd had to move out of our big house in Point-du-Fleuve. And there were no more ballet lessons. Nevertheless, we'd managed to hang on to this property. It had been in Alfie's family for generations, so the mortgage had been payed off long ago. He told his lawyer he wanted Celia to have it because he'd planned that it would be hers one day anyway. The divorce hadn't been an ugly one. Just sad. Incredibly sad.

I thought about that letter again. I couldn't help but be curious about what Alfie had to say, after all these years. And I didn't have the bitterness toward him that Celia did. But I feared reading that letter would open up a whole place in my heart I had firmly closed off years ago. I didn't know if I was ready for that. Certainly Celia wasn't.

When Alfie left, so did my illusions about true love. True love was something my parents had. But my own search had proved it more elusive than I'd imagined. I'd come to believe the German proverb was true. *With true love it's like seeing ghosts: everyone talks about it, but few have ever seen it.*

I suppose that over the years I'd decided I was better off without the question of its existence dangling over my head. Reading the letter would mean opening up all those old emotions—the disappointment, the dashed hopes, the feeling of rejection. I was about to step into my future. Did I really want to open a doorway into my past?

Celia shook her head as if to clear away the memories and handed Caleb his towel after giving it several firm shakes to rid it of sand. "Go on inside and get changed. Gramma will get you that lemonade. Let's be ready to leave for town in ten minutes, okay, baby?"

We closed the door on the tearoom, and I looked across the street at the sign for Jo-Ann's Flower Shop. Lunch had been lovely—although a bit fancy for a seven-year-old boy. But it was a celebration of sorts, and I wanted it to be special. I suppose Caleb might have been just as happy with McDonald's. However, he hadn't complained about the sandwich with a side of fries and cake for dessert at Victoria's Tearoom either. And its location, right across the street and three doors down from a certain flower shop, was convenient.

"So what's this all about, Mom? You said that cake was to celebrate. What are we celebrating?"

"Come with me." Port Sandford was busy in the summer

with all the tourists and cottagers flocking to the beaches, but it was still small town enough not to require traffic lights at many of its intersections. We walked across the street, and I swung the door open wide to the sound of the chime overhead. I'd told Jo-Ann to expect us today, and she came out from behind the counter and gave me a big hug.

She grinned widely. "Welcome, 'boss.'"

Celia's eyes darted between the two of us. "Boss?"

"Surprise!" I bit my lip.

"Oh my gracious!" Jo-Ann's hand flew to her mouth. "You hadn't told her yet?"

I laughed. "I was about to."

"So ... you own this? How? When? I'm confused." Celia turned slowly taking in the refrigerators, the prearranged bouquets, the potted plants, and the small display of gardening supplies.

"I signed the paperwork yesterday. Jo-Ann is the owner—well, was—until yesterday. She's retiring, and I'm going to take it over."

"Over time," Jo-Ann contributed. "I'll introduce her to my customers, the folks at the funeral home, our accounting program, the suppliers—everything."

I nodded. "By this time next year, Jo-Ann will fully retire, and the flower shop will be solely my responsibility." I took Celia by the hand. "Come. Have a look back here."

Celia followed, and I waved a hand at the large back room previously used only for staging the arrangements.

"This," I said, waving my hand at the space, "will be my art studio. I'm going to hold evening art classes for small groups and introduce them to watercolors and acrylics."

Celia blinked. "So your house in Point-du-Fleuve?"

I sighed. "That's the one part of the plan I don't like. I'll be moving here, and I'll have to sell the house."

Caleb walked the perimeter of the room, his fingers

brushing lightly over the vases filled with eucalyptus, baby's breath, and silver lace dusty miller.

"Don't touch," Celia scolded.

"It's okay. He can't hurt anything. Maybe he'd like to come and work with me here one day. What do you think, Caleb?"

He looked up and grinned. "Is all this really yours, Gramma?"

I nodded.

"Cool." He looked up at his mom, cupped his hand to his mouth, and made an attempt to whisper. "When do we go to the playground?"

Celia bent down and spoke to him at eye level. "In just a minute, sweetie." I couldn't read her expression.

"So, this back room. You'll still be needing it for making flower arrangements, right? How are you going to manage an art studio in here too?"

"Oh, she's got it all worked out," Jo-Ann pulled open a drawer. "She left a copy of her plans with me. Have a look." She pulled the papers out of the drawer and spread them out on the countertop.

The three of us stood side-by-side while I explained. Caleb hopped up on the counter and looked on as well. "It's going to require a bit of renovation, but nothing I can't handle with a little help from some friends."

Jack had offered his help. So had another neighbor. And Jack was still in contact with the contractor who had finished his home. He'd said he'd be willing do some of the work for a very reasonable price.

I pointed at the two pages of plans. The first was the current layout of the back room, the second was the planned design. "It's really not that complicated. See how right now, this large table takes up most of the room back here?"

Celia nodded.

"Well, a lot of space is wasted because no one really uses

what's at the center of the table, and it ends up just housing clutter—as I recall from my days working with Margie at the little shop in Point-du-Fleuve."

Jo-Ann nodded.

"I don't remember you working at a flower shop, Gramma." My grandson's eyes danced with curiosity.

"That's because that was a long time ago. Before you were born. Even before your mom was born."

His eyes grew round.

Celia laughed and put a hand on his knee. "He doesn't even know *I* had a life before he was born, let alone that Gramma had one before me." She nodded at me. "Go on, Mom."

I smoothed out the plans once more. "So, in the new design, we'll still keep all this wonderful open, brightly lit space. But we'll put smaller tables with two stools each in this section. See?" I pointed at the page with the new design. "And over here, we'll have a large island with lots of storage that backs up to the worktable here. There will still be lots of space for two or three people to work around that table. And if need be—for a big event like a wedding or funeral—we can push two of the other tables together. They're sturdy, but they'll still move around on casters—with brakes on them for when we want them stationary. And more shelving all along this wall."

I stopped and met my daughter's gaze. "Well? What do you think?"

3

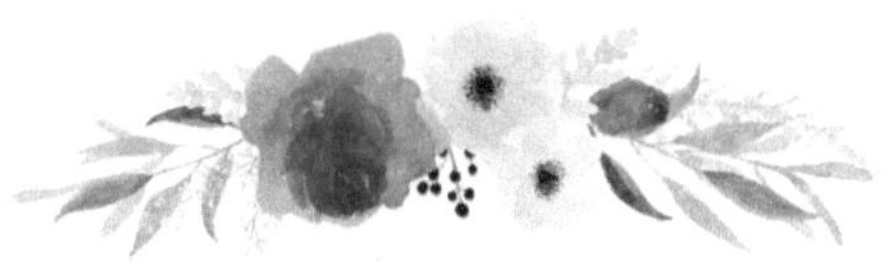

The lakeside scenery whizzed by as we drove back to the cottage, Celia in the passenger seat beside me, Caleb staring out the back window at the sandbanks. Every once in a while, there was a break in the rolling dunes with a clear view out toward the lake. Each little glimpse was a small vignette—people lying on towels in the sun, children wearing water wings and carrying pails and shovels, picnics spread out on the beach.

Every once in a while, Caleb would pipe up with a contribution from the backseat. "Did you see that, Gramma? Those people had a little black dog." Or, "I saw a kite that looked like an octopus!" His mom and I would comment that we'd seen it too, but truthfully, my focus was more on what Celia was saying.

"I still can't get over it." She shook her head. "It's going to be beautiful, Mom. I'm so happy for you."

I smiled at my daughter. I was so lucky. How many daughters would be this happy to find out their mother and occasional babysitter was moving 180 miles away?

She stared out the window for a few minutes. "I've always

15

felt bad about how many of your dreams you've had to give up."
She turned back to me, her eyes welling with tears.

"Oh, Celia." I took her hand and squeezed it.

"I mean it, Mom. After he left—" She lowered her voice and
looked over her shoulder at Caleb, who was still staring out at
the scenery. "After he left, you had to make so many sacrifices."

A familiar pang rose in my chest. I couldn't remember the
last time she'd even talked about Alfie. And she never referred
to him as "Dad." Always "he." Or words I'd rather she not say
about anyone.

"Parenting is all about sacrifices." I squeezed her hand. "You
know that."

"Sure. But you made more than I've had to make."

"It was a different time." She wasn't wrong. I just didn't like
dwelling on the past this way. Celia and I shared many things in
common. Left to face life on our own after Alfie left, we'd
grown very close. But whereas I'd learned to forgive my ex-
husband for leaving and had moved on with my life, Celia had
never healed from that wound. She was a wonderful wife and
mother, but I ached for the part of her that was missing. I had
wonderful memories of my own Papa—almost idyllic. I'd
wanted that for my daughter. And Alfie had loved her. Fiercely.

I could still remember the way he used to spread out a
blanket on the floor for Celia when she was a baby. He'd lie
down beside her. Celia would babble away at him and he'd talk
back to her as though they were having a grown-up
conversation.

I smiled at the memory, but pain came with it too. One of
those afternoons was what I remembered as the beginning of
the end of my marriage. I turned to Celia, determined not to
think about that now. Or the letter that sat at home waiting to
invite a whole floodgate of memories back into my life. Maybe
that wasn't what I needed right now. Despite my curiosity about

the first communication from my ex-husband in thirty years, I should probably just tear up the letter and throw it away.

Celia pulled her hand away and wiped at the tears. "Anyway, I'm very happy for you." She laughed. "I know we had cake at the tea shop, but I feel like we should have another one now that I know what we're celebrating."

Caleb leaned forward. "Did you say Gramma's making cake?"

I laughed. "Did you hear anything else we were talking about?

Celia looked over her shoulder nervously for a moment.

"Nope. Why? Were you talking to me?"

"Never mind, sweetheart." Celia smiled. "You just have an uncanny ear for treats."

We'd arrived at the laneway to the cottage. I turned in and parked the car and watched Caleb tear down the slope. He stopped briefly at the cottage to open the door wide to let Hershey out, and the two of them ran for the beach. I smiled at Celia as she headed down after him. I was blessed. My dreams were coming true. It definitely wasn't the time to mess with that.

I followed them down the hill, walked into the cottage, pulled up the lid on the roll top desk and held the envelope with the letter tucked inside and ran a finger over the familiar handwriting. Then I held both sides of the envelope and prepared to tear it when Celia came in the door to the cottage. "I'll get the towel," she called over her shoulder to Caleb, who evidently had found trouble already.

I tossed the letter in the trash can underneath the desk and slid the lid closed. "I'll get that towel," I said.

4

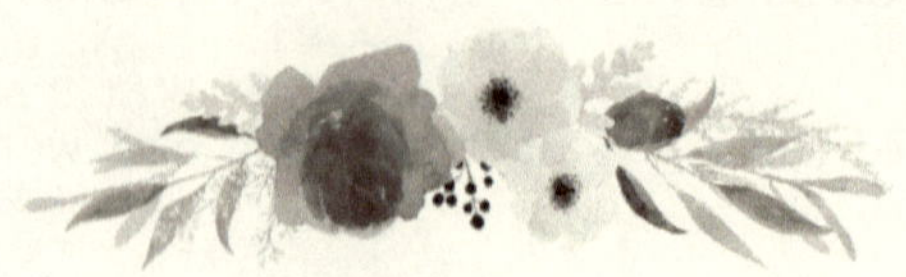

"All the dishes, Caleb. Don't forget to dry the silverware."

"I know, I know." He picked up the tea towel again and turned back to the sink.

I smirked. Celia hadn't even looked up, yet she'd known he'd walked away from his post. She'd insisted that the two of them help me clean the cottage before they left today for Point-du-Fleuve. They would be back before the summer was over after taking care of some family commitments and a soccer match or two in the next couple of weeks.

"I can do this all myself after you're gone," I told her. "Why not let Caleb spend one last morning playing by the beach?"

"Then all your towels will be wet and sandy again, and I've just cleaned them." Celia stood at the table in the breakfast nook folding the towels into neat piles while I, on her orders, sat across from her, drinking the cup of peppermint tea she'd made me. "Besides, you're a business owner now. You have lots of responsibilities."

"Not until after the weekend. Jo-Ann and I agreed I wouldn't start to learn the ropes until after you two are gone.

18

And ..." I looked up at her. "There's something I haven't told you."

Celia stopped mid-fold. "More surprises?"

"I suppose you could say that. It certainly surprised me."

Celia sat down. "What, Mom? Spill it."

"Well, when I was on my way home from the shop the day that I signed all the paperwork to take over the business, I met my neighbor, Jack."

"Jack. You mean Mr. Murphy? A few doors down, right? He and his wife built that huge cottage when they retired?"

"Yes, well Emma died quite a few years ago now. Cancer."

Celia's eyes widened. "I didn't know. I never heard."

I nodded. "Anyway, Jack was an investment lawyer, you know. Before he retired."

"Okay ..."

"So, he's been giving me some advice here and there on my business plan. He's offered to help with the renovations and get some friends to help too." I watched Celia's face for her reaction. A moment ago, she didn't even know Jack's wife had died. What would she think of my going out on a date with him? I wasn't even sure how I felt about it yet. The whole thing felt so sudden and out of nowhere.

"Well?" Celia sat with a towel in her lap, the two ends still clutched in either hand.

"Well, He's been very supportive. And when I came home the other day, I met him in the laneway. He was out for a walk with Pepper—their Cocker Spaniel."

"Mom, out with it. What's the surprise?"

I took a sip of the tea. "Well, it's not so much of a surprise, I suppose. It's just that I was surprised by it."

"By what?" Celia's eyes sparked with recognition. "He asked you out on a date, didn't he?"

I nodded.

"Oh, Mom, that's wonderful."

"You really think so?" A flush had crept into my cheeks.

"I do. He's a nice man from what I remember and obviously financially stable."

"Celia!" I took the last sip of tea and reached across the table for one of the towels and started folding. "It's not as though we're getting married. This is a first date. In fact, I don't even know if I should call it a date. He just wanted to celebrate my success with me."

"You can't fool me," she said. "Just look at you. You're like the proverbial smitten schoolgirl. When is he taking you out? What are you going to wear?"

I waved my hand at her. "Tonight. And I don't know. I haven't decided. I wasn't going to get that wound up about it until you—"

"Until I what? Got excited for you? Of course I'm excited for you. You're starting this business, you're moving down here to look at this every day." She gestured to the lakefront. "And now you have a love interest. What is there not to be excited about?"

Caleb finished at the sink and headed for his bedroom.

"Wait a minute, young man. Everything finished?"

"All of them, Mom. Just like you said." Energy fairly escaped through his fingertips and toes.

"Just let him go outside for a little while," I whispered across the table.

Celia ignored me. "You can go outside in a minute. Just empty the trash first. All the rooms. The bags are under the kitchen sink. Take a big bag and you can dump all the trash cans into it. Got it?"

"Got it." Caleb said, his voice deflated.

"Hard taskmaster." I winked playfully at my daughter.

"You sure are different as Gramma than you were as Mom."

I shrugged. "My job description has changed. This one, I just get to spoil."

Caleb dragged the garbage bag from room to room, while

Celia finished folding towels. She looked around. "I guess I should go and strip the beds and start a load of the sheets."

"Or you could sit down for a minute and enjoy another cup of tea with me." I held up my empty teacup.

Caleb ran into the room. "Gramma, Gramma. Can I have this stamp?" The garbage bag trailed behind him and in his hand, he held an envelope. *The* envelope. With *the* letter inside it.

I stood and almost knocked over the teacup. "Oh that. Sure, dear. You can have it." I held up the envelope, making sure the reverse side faced Celia. "Go get the scissors so I can cut it out for you." I did my best to keep my voice steady. I dared not look in Celia's direction for fear the look on my face would give me away.

"It's Lightning McQueen, Mom. Look." He bent the stamp end of the envelope toward her, nearly wrenching it from my hand.

"Really? On a stamp?" Celia looked closer. "Oh, that's not a Canadian stamp, sweetie. It's from America." Her eyes met mine in a question.

I grabbed Caleb's hand. "Here, honey. I'll help you. Let's go get the scissors together."

"You're not going to cut the stamp, are you, Gramma?"

"No, dear. I'll be careful to cut around it."

I pulled the scissors out of the knife block on the counter and cut around the stamp. In the vacant space, I spied a couple of words from the letter inside. Celia's name, for one. A pang of emotion stabbed at my heart.

Alfie had left. And he had been an absentee father. I was justified in feeling that I owed him nothing. But did I really intend to leave this letter unanswered, when he might merely be wanting to know about his daughter? Was I that heartless ... to withhold whatever information was easily within my power to give him?

At the same time, I knew Celia wouldn't want me to have anything to do with her father. But this wasn't Celia's letter. Alfie wrote it to me.

I handed Caleb the stamp and he held out the garbage bag. "Here, Gramma, you can throw that away now."

"You know, on second thought, I might hang on to this a while longer."

He shrugged. "Okay."

But I'd read it later. After my date with Jack. I was distracted enough as it was.

5

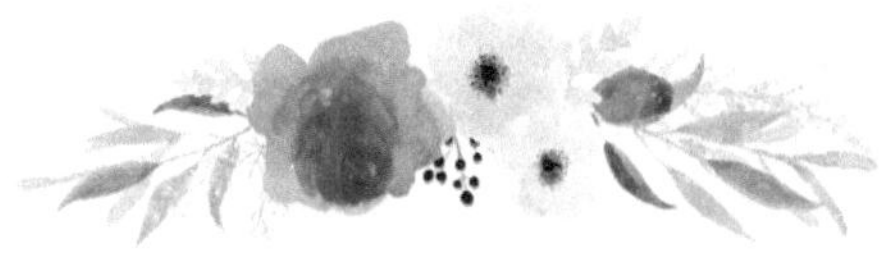

The summer after Alfie and I married was the first time I'd come to Port Sandford. At that time, his father owned the stretch of lakefront land which had been purchased by Alfie's grandfather years before. I'd fallen in love with the lake that year. Coming from Point-du-Fleuve, a small town in Quebec along the Ottawa River, I knew what living near water was like. But something about Lake Ontario was magical to me. I couldn't conceive of a lake so big one couldn't see the other side. I'd never seen an ocean either, but I couldn't imagine it being more wonderful than this place. In my memories of that first summer, Lake Ontario was all endless blue sparkling water beneath an equally endless sky.

Back then there was no cottage on the property. Alfie and I pitched a tent and spent a lovely week swimming and eating over a campfire. Two years later, Alfie's father passed away, leaving him the plot of land. At first, Alfie thought of selling it. We needed the money, and we had a home in Point-du-Fleuve. But we decided to build a seasonal cottage. We'd imagined years surrounded by the joyful laughter of our children, sharing with them our love for the lake.

Unfortunately, although the cottage remained a part of Celia's summers for her entire life, the rest of the dream failed to come true. In the meantime, Port Sandford grew from a small, close-knit community of people who'd lived there most of their lives into a tourist destination. The beach and the sandbanks of course were the largest attractions, but the Chamber of Commerce had worked hard to keep the quaint downtown full of thriving businesses that held their own attraction for locals and "summer people" alike. And over the last number of years, business opportunities in Port Sandford had become increasingly attractive to a younger, hipper set who adopted our small town in the hopes of living a simpler life outside of Toronto.

The Blue Oyster, the chic new restaurant Jack took me to for our celebration was one such business, started by a young couple who'd moved to Port Sandford just six months before. Yet the fledgling establishment had earned several favorable reviews from the local press as well as online food review sites. So it was no easy feat that Jack had managed to reserve us a table for that evening. He'd chosen a quiet little corner, "so we can talk."

We both decided on Roast Beef Tenderloin with Cognac Butter and sides of Carrot Mash with Crème Fraîche and Shredded Brussels Sprouts with Slow-Fried Shallots and Jack ordered an appetizer and a bottle of champagne.

"Champagne?"

He grinned. "I told you I'd order their best bottle. It's a celebration, isn't it?" He raised his glass. "To new beginnings. And to the success of Every Bloomin' Thing!" he said.

I laughed before I could take a sip. "That sounded so funny."

He grinned. "Well, I'll admit it didn't come out quite the way I imagined. But I mean it, Adele. I wish you success in everything you do. I think you're really onto something with your flower-store-by-day, painting-studio-by-night idea."

I took a sip of the champagne and stared at the dancing flame of the candle on the table. For a moment, I briefly wondered what Alfie would think of it. The thought surprised me. Of course, for years after our divorce, I would think those kinds of thoughts. But it had been years since I had wondered about his opinions regarding my life. That letter had started my thoughts turning to him again. That letter that waited once again in the roll top desk. I'd forced myself not to think about it since Caleb had rescued it from the trash, and I'd promised myself I'd wait until after tonight to revisit the idea of whether or not I should read it. But here I was wondering about my ex-husband and his opinions. Of course I knew he'd be proud of me. He'd always loved my paintings. When Celia was little, I'd often paint while she napped.

The candle flickered as the waiter approached and served us our appetizer, the restaurant's signature dish: Oysters with Bacon Mignonette.

"You okay?" Jack's brow furrowed.

I smiled. "It's nothing. Just old memories."

Jack looked around. "In this place? What did it used to be, anyway? I can't remember. Before these folks bought it, wasn't it empty for a season?"

"I think you're right. Wasn't it the fish and chips place?"

"Captain Poppie's?" Jack turned around in his seat. "You know, I think you're right. How could I have forgotten? We used to come here all the time."

"You and Emma?"

Jack blushed. I couldn't imagine why. Thinking of Emma was even more natural than my thinking of Alfie. For years we'd get together—at my place when Celia was tucked in her own bed or theirs when she slept over at at Sarah's or another friend's—for games night. Emma – or I – would brew a pot of coffee, and we'd pull out the board games or a deck of cards. Sometimes another neighbor or two would join our get-togethers, but the three of us had been a staple. Emma and I had known each other since the day I delivered a loaf of banana bread not long after they first moved in. We were soon fast friends. As far as games night was concerned, I always figured the two of them felt sorry for me spending my evenings alone while Celia was tucked in her bunk, exhausted from a day spent in the wind, waves, and sand. They weren't wrong. I gladly accepted the companionship.

"I miss her," I said. "She was a wonderful woman."

"She was." Jack shifted in his chair and took another sip of his champagne. I guessed he was feeling about as awkward as I was. I didn't know much about whether or not Jack had found female companionship since Emma's passing, but dating was new for me. When I was raising Celia, she was my world. And since then ... well, I'd given up on any notions of true love long ago. They'd died when Alfie left. I never expected to resurrect them at all, let alone now that I was long past the age of first dates and romance. And now here I sat with an old friend who shared memories of his wife with me. After all these years, did I imagine this was where I'd find love? Maybe I should have insisted on making dinner and having him over to the cottage. A piece of bumbleberry pie and some ice cream could have made just as good a celebration between friends.

Jack lifted his seafood fork. "Let's dig in to these oysters, shall we?"

I smiled. "Okay. I'll follow your lead?"

Jack lowered his fork and stared at me. "You've never eaten an oyster?"

I shook my head.

"Well, you're in for a treat," he said. He dug around with his fork. "You have to move the oyster around in the half shell to make sure it's detached. Like this, see? Then you put down your fork, pick up the shell, and with the wide end to your mouth, you just tip it back ..." He chewed a moment. "Chew and swallow."

"Like this?" I poked around nervously with the little fork.

"You don't have to chew very much. It's very soft and sort of —well—slides down your throat. It's raw, you see."

"Raw?' I shivered and Jack laughed.

"It's an experience. Try it."

I put the fork down and drew the oyster to my mouth. "It smells good ..."

"Go ahead," he urged, his eyebrows raised and his mouth hanging open a little, like a parent feeding a baby.

I had to laugh at that image and took the oyster away from my mouth.

Jack laughed again. "Go ahead. Just let it slide down. Oh wait." He leaned across the table and touched my oyster. Turn it around. You want the wide end toward your mouth. It's more aerodynamic that way."

"Aerodynamic?"

"For lack of a better word."

I closed my eyes, tipped the oyster, and felt the cool slipperiness of it. I chewed two times and, like Jack said, let it slide down my throat. "You know, it's okay."

"Just okay?"

"Not bad."

"You can do better than that. You tasted the saltiness?"

"Of course." I took another half shell from the serving plate.

"Would you say there's sweetness?"

I considered that. "A little. But is that the bacon in the sauce or the oyster?"

"Some people say the oysters themselves can have a sweet taste. I think these are a little that way. You can also describe oysters as 'Melony, or buttery, coppery, or briny.'"

"Buttery I can understand. Better than saying slimy."

Jack laughed and took a sip of champagne. "Well, you tried. I've always admired that about you, Adele. You don't back down from a challenge. Like this new adventure of yours."

I lowered my head. It was nice, spending this time with Jack, but it was hard to move him in my mind from Emma's husband and my friend to this new role he seemed interested in assuming.

He put his champagne flute down on the table.

"How soon do you envision starting the art classes?"

I picked up my napkin and dabbed it on my lips. I had the sensation that the slimy oyster was dripping everywhere, although I was quite certain it was my imagination.

"Well not right away. I want to give myself a chance to get to know the business through Jo-Ann's eyes and learn what she can teach me. She needs to take me in detail through all the bookkeeping procedures. I have to learn that fancy digital cash register and her tracking system for orders. And get the layout of her shop on a busy day, like when she's working on wedding or funeral arrangements."

I stared at the flickering candle, but my view was the vision of the shop the way I imagined it. "Probably in the new year, I'll start putting classes together. It would be great to do it in September. Everyone's thinking about new starts and learning new things when their kids are off to school. But I couldn't possibly be ready to start then."

Jack picked up the oyster half shells from his plate and put them back on the serving plate, turned upside down. I followed suit.

"What's that for?"

"You don't have to do it. It's just a courtesy to the server. Let's them know you're finished with them."

Jack's world was so different from mine. He and Emma had experienced so many things I'd never experienced. But they'd never made me feel inadequate or less-than. I wondered briefly how different my life would have been if I'd followed any of the other paths that at one time seemed open to me. If Alfie and I had somehow stayed married. Or even if I'd married my high school sweetheart, Frank. Thoughts of Alfie reminded me again of the letter that waited at home for me. I still hadn't decided whether or not to read it.

"You okay? Those oysters disagreeing with you?"

I shook my head and forced a smile. "I'm fine."

"So, have you thought about which of your paintings you're going to hang in the shop?"

I smiled. I had. "I've been working away at a whole series of watercolors—a few acrylics—of the town and the sandbanks across the seasons. I figure I'll hang them as they're seasonally appropriate. I know they'll sell well with tourists and locals."

"I agree. That sounds like a great idea. You'll hang those right away, then?"

"I think so." I'd been trying to figure this out myself. "I know Jo-Ann is supportive of my vision for the business. It just feels a little irreverent to walk in and take over right away."

Jack nodded. "I understand. Give yourself a little time, like you said, and you'll get a sense for how to go forward. Jo-Ann seems really easy-going. It may not be as hard as you think." He took a sip of his champagne. "But it would be a shame to miss out on the whole summer tourist season."

Just then our server arrived, took away the oyster plate and returned a moment later with our entrees. Jack reached for his knife and fork, "Bon appetite."

I took a bite of the beef tenderloin. "It's very good."

Jack nodded. "It's cooked just right. I'm very glad you agreed to come with me tonight, Adele. I've been looking for an excuse to do this for some time now."

I almost choked.

"At first, I was afraid summer was going to get away on me, and I wouldn't work up the courage to ask you." He smiled. "So when you brought me your business plan and told me you intended to stay here year-round, I was delighted. And I figured this celebration was just the excuse I was looking for." He reached across the table and took my hand as he continued to gaze into my eyes.

I suddenly felt there wasn't enough air in the room. I pulled my hand away and dabbed again with the napkin. "Jack, I—"

"It's okay. This is all new. You probably didn't know I had feelings for you this way. I'm not expecting you to reciprocate at this moment. But I believe in being forthright, so I wanted to let you know my intentions. I intend to court you, Adele Hanson." He lifted the champagne flute once more. "To new beginnings indeed."

6

———

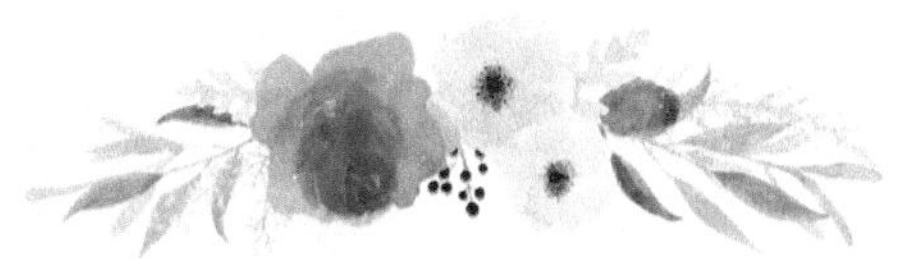

I rolled over and faced the sunlight streaming over my bed. Whenever I stayed at the cottage, I liked to leave the curtains open to be wakened by the natural light. But I rarely slept this late. And this would be the last morning of my free and easy life. It was Sunday and tomorrow was the first day I'd spend at the flower shop. A tingle of excitement propelled me out of bed.

Once in the kitchen, I realized how eerily quiet the cottage seemed without Celia and Caleb here. Through the years, I'd spent less time here alone than they had. Celia would often bring Caleb here on summer holidays while I still had work at the insurance office in Point-du-Fleuve. But this morning, there was only me and my overwhelming thoughts about my date with Jack last night. And the letter.

I pulled my mug from the cupboard and swirled the coffee in the pot of the coffee maker. It had been set to turn on automatically earlier this morning and had sat a little longer than I usually let it. No matter. I needed it strong this morning. I walked to the roll top desk.

Jack had been the perfect gentleman at dinner and our

conversation had been stimulating. I learned something new every time we talked. He was funny and charming. But somewhere between the beef tenderloin and the tiramisu for dessert, I had decided I would definitely read Alfie's letter. I withdrew it from the desk and clutched it as I returned to the coffee maker, poured myself a cup of coffee and headed to the big, open family room where I curled up on one of the overstuffed sofas to read.

I fingered the thinning fabric on the sofa. I suppose I'd have to replace this set with the ones in my home in Point-du-Fleuve, but I would be sad to let these go. They'd held many a sleepover guest and endured years of sand tracked in by little feet. They'd been here when Alfie was here. No one else would care, but it felt like a sad milestone nonetheless.

I lifted the flap on the envelope, pulled the letter out, and I began to read.

Dear Adele,

I know I'm probably the last person you ever expected to hear from. It's been a long time. Too long. I should never have let this much water pass under the bridge before writing to you. I've spent a lot of time the last while thinking about all the things I should have done differently.

A tear fell and I swiped at it with the sleeve of my pajamas. I could hear the cadence of Alfie's deliberate way in his words.

I want to ask a lot of questions. I've wondered how you are. How Celia is. Whether she's married. Or whether you are.

But of course, I don't even know if you'll get this letter. And I feel like I owe you a lot of explaining first. I wrote to you at the cottage address because I thought—well, I hoped—you'd have held onto that, even if you might not still be at the same address in Point-du-Fleuve.

He was right of course. The beautiful house we'd moved into after we were married was too much for just Celia and me. And too much mortgage on the paycheck I received after I found a job as a secretary, first at a logging company—a rival one of the one Alfie had worked for as a tree feller—and later at McClelland's Insurance. We'd moved into a much smaller home in town. Celia took the bus to school, and I walked the several blocks to work in the summer, and a colleague picked me up on her way to work in the winter until I was able to afford a used car.

I know it's selfish of me, but I think I wanted to make sure you had the cottage not just for you but for me too. Over the years, I've pictured you there. And Celia. It was comforting to think I knew where you'd be and that part of me, somehow, was with you.

More tears fell. From my window, the lake lay relatively calm. This lake—the scene of so many beautiful memories— was one of the few constants in my life, despite the changes that the years had seen. I had been grateful for this place. So had Celia. Somewhere along the way it had become ours—just the two of us. And yet it bore the mark of Alfie in every beam and every nail, since he'd built the whole thing himself from plans we'd sketched together at the kitchen table in that first house in Point-du-Fleuve.

I'm living in Chattanooga. I've been in a lot of other places between the time I left and now but if you don't mind, I don't really want to tell about all that yet. I'll just center in on the last few years and what's been going on here since that's the part that really matters.

I came here just about four years ago. Like most places I've been during all these years, I came for the work. Work had pretty much dried up where I'd been staying, and a buddy of mine had a friend here who could get us both a place on a construction crew.

Two years ago I started driving a truck for the same reason, but I'm still based out of Chattanooga.

Anyway, one of the first construction projects we had was this church here. During breaks, the padre—Pastor Manuel—would come out and bring the guys donuts or sandwiches and coffee. Real nice guy. Real down to earth. He and I got to talking, and well, I guess a lot of what he said made sense to me. One day after work, I stayed to talk with the padre. Eventually, I started going to services at the church.

I've come to believe that I'm forgiven by God of all the wrong things I've done in my life. That's important. I know it is. Still, I know I need to ask you to forgive me too.

There's nothing I would like more than to hear from you, but I'm not going to ask that of you. It's been a long time, and you owe me nothing. You don't even owe me your forgiveness. But I'm asking anyway.

I hope you are well and happy and that Celia is too. I wish you everything good, Adele.

Love, Alfie

I was barely able to read the last words, the tears were flowing so freely by then. The letter was brief, but there had been far more in it than I'd imagined. I'd need to think long and hard about it because, at this moment, I wanted more than anything to write him back. Was that crazy? My brain seemed abuzz with a confusion of thoughts.

I folded the letter and laid it on the coffee table and headed down the hall to the bathroom for a tissue when I heard a knock on the door. "Just a minute," I called out and ran toward my bedroom instead, snatched my robe from the hook on the back of the door and pulled it hastily around me. I stopped briefly in the bathroom to splash water on my face and shake my head at the sorry reflection: red, puffy eyes and bedhead.

I headed for the big, wooden front door when I realized the

knock had come from the back door that led to the beach. I turned and stared through the open glass at the image of Jack, who had turned and was facing out toward the water while he waited. I followed his line of vision to see Pepper several yards away, digging furiously for treasure on the beach.

I opened the door. "Good morning," I said, realizing even as I did these were the first words I'd spoken to anyone today. My voice was hoarse. I cleared my throat.

Jack's eyes widened as he took in the picture I presented. "Adele, my goodness, are you okay?"

I nodded. "It's okay. I slept late and then ..." How could I explain my emotional state? "What brings you by? Care to come in for a cup of coffee? It's fresh."

Jack shuffled and looked out toward the lake. "I was just out for my morning walk. I thought you might like to join me. But I can come by another time."

I shook my head. "It's okay. Give me just a minute to get dressed and run a brush through my hair. A walk sounds lovely." I needed something to clear my head.

We walked along the beach between our two properties. Jack's was at the end of our laneway, the beach prevented from going any further down the shore by a massive outcropping of rocks that jutted out into the lake. To further preserve their privacy, Jack and Emma had bought acres of land surrounding their place. So from the beach in front of his house, we walked along a well-worn path through the woods. We were only a few feet in when I heard the distinct hum of a mosquito in my ear.

I swatted. "Forgot bug spray."

Jack's brow furrowed. "You okay?"

I laughed. Bug spray was standard issue around here in the summer, and no Canadian cottager in their right mind ventured out without it. Between the image that greeted him at the door this morning and forgetting that cardinal rule, it was no wonder he was concerned.

"Just a lot on my mind, is all."

"Not having any regrets, I hope. I mean, it's natural if you are. But your plan is solid, Adele. You don't need to worry."

I shook my head. "It's not that. I'm actually excited to get started tomorrow."

"Good," he said and slipped his hand into mine, interlocking our fingers.

My head swam. I hadn't yet processed what had transpired between us last night nor Alfie's letter this morning. I felt wildly out of control. But I wasn't a teenaged schoolgirl, and this wasn't some adolescent summer fling. I cared too much about Jack to enter into something without thinking it through.

I swatted again. "You know, I don't know that I'm going to be able to go much further without that bug spray. I think I should head back. I've got a lot to do to get ready for tomorrow, anyway." That last part was a lie. I'd been ready for weeks. But with all the conflicting thoughts swirling around in my brain, it was the only thing I could come up with.

Jack turned on the path and started heading the other way. "No problem."

"Raincheck?"

"Of course. How about tomorrow after dinner? You can tell me all about your first day of work." He grinned. "I'll bring the bug spray."

7

———

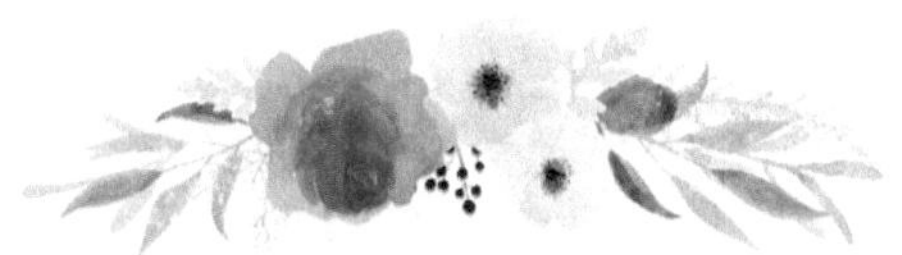

Jo-Ann greeted me at the door with a mug of coffee, a stack of files, and her laptop computer.

"Oh boy." I took the coffee from her and peeked inside the first file folder on the stack. "You don't mess around."

"Well, I may as well bring you up to speed as quickly as possible. I want you to succeed at this as much as you do."

She was right. I'd been planning for this day for months, and I hoped to get myself acquainted with all aspects of the business as soon as possible so I could begin to take them over, allowing Jo-Ann more and more freedom to enjoy her retirement. It would also allow me more and more control over the future direction of Every Bloomin' Thing. I'd just never imagined how confused I'd feel about every other part of my life during the process. It would take work to push the emotional rollercoaster of the weekend to the side and concentrate on accounting. At the same time, work was a welcome distraction.

Jo-Ann led me to the back room where we she had set two stools side by side at the large table. "My niece Tina will watch the shop for us. The weather's too nice outside for too many

37

customers to be coming in today, and we won't start getting ready for the weekend's weddings until later in the week. Tina's looking over the inventory and preparing our order for that." She patted the seat beside her and opened up her laptop.

"You mentioned that everything to do with the shop you manage through some software, isn't that right?" I pulled my glasses from my handbag to peer at the computer screen.

"That's right. It's brilliant. All your inventory, your invoices, payroll, your proposals for weddings or events—it's all right in this little baby." She tapped the computer. "Even website design if you wanted, but we have someone local who takes care of that for us."

"Wow. So different from when I worked at the shop in Point-du-Fleuve with Margie." I could still picture that quaint little shop in our small town nestled on the Quebec side of the Ottawa river. Margie had started as my boss and became my mentor and my friend. I would never have survived my breakup with Frank if it hadn't been for her offering me that job. And of course, I would never have met Alfie at all. Over the years, I'd been tempted to wonder whether that would have been a good thing, but then there would have been no Celia, and she was part of my life I had no regrets about.

Jo-Ann touched my arm with a reassuring nudge. "Don't worry. If I can do this, you can handle it. No problem."

We sat on those stools until our bottoms were numb while Jo-Ann led me through her accounting program. She'd shown me the books long ago, as part of our original discussions prior to my signing on the dotted line, and I'd seen her worn accounting folders where she kept physical copies of invoices, receivables, and receipts. Now she took me into the inner work-ings of those things so I could be the one responsible for it all.

Jo-Ann closed the lid on the computer and turned to me. "That's enough of that for now. My head is spinning from all those numbers, and my body is stiff from sitting too long. Let's get a coffee and visit a little while." I followed her ample frame as she marched out to the front of the shop. "Tina, sweetie, you go on and take a break. Why don't you go to the coffee shop down the street and get yourself something or ..." She glanced at her watch. "Goodness, get yourself some lunch. I had no idea we'd been sitting there so long."

Tina grabbed her handbag and headed for the door. "Okay, Aunt Jo-Ann. Need anything?"

"Not me. You, Adele?"

I shook my head. I had picked up a catalogue for an international flower service from under the counter and was leafing through it. "Do you receive many orders through this service?"

Jo-Ann shook her head. "More and more people from longer distances order through our website rather than paying the premium for one of those arrangements." She shrugged. "They know their arrangement will be bigger and look like they spent more if they order directly."

"Makes sense." I was just putting the catalogue away when the bell over the door chimed and in walked a man with a stocky frame, wearing sunglasses and a baseball cap. Silhouetted against the sun, the moment matched one from more than thirty years ago, and immediately a flood of memories rushed in.

The memory rushed back, fully alive, as though it were yesterday. A man had walked into Marge's flower shop then and taken off his sunglasses as he bent to study a pre-made bouquet in one of the pails of water at the front of the shop. He moved to the refrigerator, opened the door and picked out a long-stemmed rose. He sniffed it and replaced it in its pail of water. I knew most of the people in Point-du-Fleuve, but I'd never seen this man before. Standing behind the counter on days we had no weddings or funerals to prepare for, Margie and I often made a game of guessing a customer's needs when we spotted them approaching the door of the shop. First Date. Proud Grandparent. Grieving Friend. Repentant Husband. This man: undoubtedly First Date material.

I took a few steps in his direction. "Can I help you with anything?"

The customer looked up, relief written on his face. "Uh, yeah. I'm lookin' for …"

He stopped as his eyes met mine. He smiled, removed his cap, and opened his mouth as though to say more, but no words came out.

I smiled. "Maybe it would help if you told me who the flowers are for. It is flowers you're looking for, yes?"

The man looked down briefly and cleared his throat, then his eyes met mine again. Steel blue. Framed by a strong jaw and a disarming smile. "I … uh … you'll have to excuse me. I never expected to find something more beautiful in here than the flowers."

A deep blush rose in my cheeks and something fell over in the back of the shop. I could picture Margie straining for a better view.

"Oh. I … uh … well, thank you." I ran nervous fingers through my hair and tucked it behind my ear. "Is there anything I can help you with?"

He fingered the baseball cap. "Sorry. Didn't mean to embarrass you. That probably sounded like a line."

I giggled. "It kind of did."

"I meant it, though."

I blushed again and shook my head. This time it was my mouth that opened with no sound coming out.

More noises from the back room.

"Well then." The man shuffled a little, cleared his throat once more. He looked around the shop before continuing. "A close friend died."

"Oh. I'm so sorry to hear that." It was routine in the flower business to offer condolences. We dealt with people at their most joyful moments—weddings, birthdays, the arrival of new lives. And at their most difficult—illnesses and deaths.

So maybe I felt bad about pegging him as First Date when in fact he was Grieving Friend. I'm not sure what I was thinking. Before I knew what I was doing, I had reached out and touched the man's arm. Electricity ran through me, followed by another awkward silence as we gazed into each other's eyes.

I cringed at the thought of what Margie would say when the man left the shop. I stepped back, moving in the direction of the cashier counter. "You're ... uh ... looking for a funeral arrangement then?" I'd show the man the photo album with our selection. There had to be a way to put this encounter back on some sort of professional footing. "We can send an arrangement directly to the funeral home in town or make arrangements to have one sent to several of the neighboring towns as well—as far away as Hull—but not across the border into Ontario, unfortunately."

The man looked around the shop again. "Not for the funeral. No, um, this friend died a while ago."

I raised an eyebrow. "Oh?" There was something oddly offhand about the way he said that. Maybe I hadn't been wrong about this man's original intentions for entering the shop after all.

"Uh ... yeah. I was thinkin' something to lay at the graveside."

"Oh. I see." I kicked myself. Grieving after all. This man had me completely off-balance.

But I was behind the counter now. Him on the other side. I pulled out the photo album of our selection of arrangements and began paging through. I found one I thought might be suitable and pointed to it. "Something like this then?"

"Yeah. Sure. That's great."

I looked up. He hadn't even glanced at the photograph. His

eyes bore into mine, as though he could see my soul, read my thoughts. I swallowed. "Just give me a few minutes."

"Alfie."

"I beg your pardon?"

"My name's Alfie."

"Okay ..."

"For the card." He motioned to the display of cards in the rack.

"Oh, there's not usually a card with this kind of arrangement, sir ..."

He smiled that beguiling smile again.

"Oh. I see ... Alfie, then."

Normally I took pleasure in putting together an arrangement in front of the customer, letting them see it take shape along with me, checking that the selection of flowers was just what they wanted. But I'd never felt a customer's scrutiny as I did now. My hands shook and my heart pounded. I finished the arrangement—not my best—and turned it toward him. "What do you think. Will this do?"

Again he nodded, barely glancing at the flowers. He paid, took the bouquet and strode to the door. The bell overhead jangled again. He turned back with a smile. "And your name? I forgot to ask."

I smiled. Because now I knew. This man was definitely first date material. "Adele," I called, and the door swung shut.

"Adele?" Jo-Ann chuckled. "Where did you go? Did you hear what I said?"

I smiled. "I'm sorry. My mind was elsewhere."

"Apparently." She motioned beside me. "I'm just going to ring this gentleman's purchase through. How about I give you your first lesson on the cash register?"

"Great." I moved aside, and Jo-Ann squeezed by and commandeered the cash register. I glanced up at the man who had inspired the memory of Alfie. Close up, he bore no resemblance at all to my ex-husband. I smiled, feeling somewhat embarrassed, although there was no way he could know the trick my mind had played.

"There are separate codes for gift items and flowers and such, but since this is a fresh-cut flower arrangement, we're going to use the 'eight' button and then this button right here. That shows that it's fresh-cut flowers. Now we're going to enter in the dollar amount." Jo-Ann pushed more buttons. "Then this POU button right here, and then the subtotal button. The cash register automatically calculates the tax. This gentleman is going to pay by cash, so we'll just enter the dollar amount— never use the decimal—and then just punch in this button right here for 'amount tendered' and the display shows us we owe him five dollars and thirty cents." She deftly scooped the change from the tray and handed it to the man with a smile.

"Thank you," he said.

"Thank *you*. You have a nice day." Jo-Ann turned to me as soon as the door swung closed behind the man. "You need that coffee worse than I thought you did. Let me get it fixed right now."

I followed Jo-Ann to the back room where she stood at the counter, scooped coffee grounds into the filter, and started the machine. I was tempted to explain myself. But what would I say? It had been years since such a vivid memory of Alfie had captured me that way. That letter he'd sent had been a distraction since it arrived.

Nevertheless, I'd reached a decision. I would write Alfie back. I had to answer his letter and put all of this to rest.

The supper dishes put away and the counter and tabletop cleared off, I sat down at the roll top desk and faced Alfie's letter. Somewhere in the desk, I had some stationery. I still wrote my own Christmas cards every year, but I couldn't remember the last time I'd written an actual letter.

I fished through the cubbies in the desk and came up with a piece of flowered paper that might well have been around when Alfie still was. I sat with my pen poised over it when I heard a knock at the door.

From my spot at the desk I could see straight to the back door where Jack stood, waving.

"The sunset is spectacular this evening," he said as soon as I opened the door. "I think you'll want to bring your camera."

Our walk. I'd forgotten all about it.

"Will I need a sweater?"

Jack nodded. "I think so."

Despite the heat of the day, evening was usually cool by the lake. It was one of the things I loved about this place. I touched a beam by the door as I walked out, thinking of Alfie's words in the letter, *Over the years, I've pictured you there. And Celia. It was comforting to think I knew where you'd be and that part of me, somehow, was with you.*

I'd imagined that years ago I had closed a door in my life. Had I, in fact, left it hanging wide open?

I closed the door of the cottage now, pulled my sweater around me, and pulled the camera strap over my neck. "You're right," I said to Jack. "The sunset is gorgeous."

8

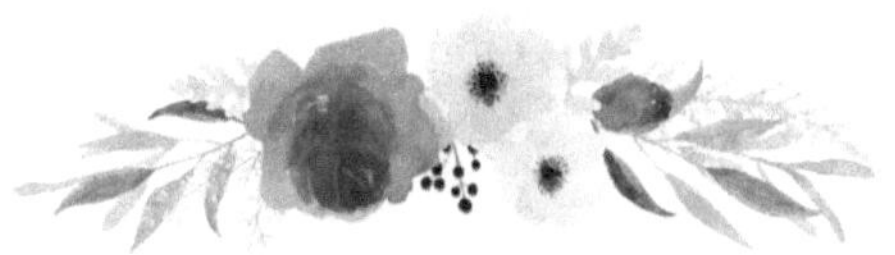

"How was your first day as shop owner?"

I peered through the lens of the camera and framed the shot so the lake occupied the lower third of the picture, the sky dominating the rest. I snapped several shots and pulled the camera away. "Well, I didn't feel like the one in charge. There's so much to learn."

"That's why you were wise to give yourself so much time to transition in and Jo-Ann to transition out."

I nodded. "That's for sure." Pepper ran down and met the waves, scurrying in and out of the water as they washed in and receded, looking, no doubt, for a crayfish or clam to claim as his prize. I lifted my camera again and caught a picture of his antics. Then two more of the sunset. I could picture that sunset on my canvas. New Gamboge for the yellow hues of the sun, with some Cadmium Red mixed in to create the fiery orange that intensified near the horizon. Then a touch of Burnt Sienna where the sky met the water and higher in the sky next to the clouds. "Thanks for suggesting I bring my camera."

It was, truly, a remarkable sunset, but more than that, it

45

gave me something to do with my hands. So Jack wouldn't be tempted to hold them.

His advance had been sweet, and I couldn't deny there had been a spark when he touched me, but I hadn't yet wrapped my head around any of this. I needed things to slow down, which was going to be difficult if we continued to see each other every day like this.

Almost as though he read my mind, Jack turned to me. "How long are you going to stay?"

"Stay?"

"I mean, you have to list your house and pack up everything, right?"

"Right." I sighed. "I'm really not looking forward to that. I'm not a pack rat or anything, but there's a lot more in that house than will fit in the cottage." And a lot more memories it would be hard to leave behind.

Jack nodded. "I hear you. I remember when we moved out here."

I smiled. Jack and Emma's "cottage" was easily three times the size of mine. Although to be fair, their house in Toronto had no doubt been even larger than that. They'd had four children living in it with them at one point, after all.

"I could help. It's not like I've got anything pressing scheduled."

"Oh no," I said, perhaps a little too hastily. "I'll have Celia."

Pepper ran up to me, a sandy piece of driftwood in his mouth, and dropped it at my feet.

Jack laughed, the lines around his brown eyes wrinkling pleasantly. "You're the designated fetch player this evening, it seems."

I picked up the stick and threw it out toward the waves. "I want to stay a week or two. I'd like to get a handle on the scope of things at the shop, help out with a wedding or two, and establish a firmer timeline with Jo-Ann about how we'll transition things. And of course, Celia and Caleb will be coming back before school starts again. But the real estate agent says the fall is the best time to list. So I can't let it wait too long."

Jack stared out toward the sunset. "You should take a picture now. The sun looks so huge when it sits at the horizon like that, doesn't it?"

"You're right," I said from behind the lens. "There's a moment that's just perfect. You don't want to miss it." I snapped several more shots as the sun seemed to expand at the horizon and get brighter. Then the moment was gone.

I lowered the camera and was startled to see that Jack was standing right beside me.

"I don't want to miss that perfect moment with you, Adele. I can see you need some time. I want to give you that. But I also don't want to miss out altogether. Don't forget that I'm here, okay?"

"Okay," I said, my voice barely above a whisper.

"I'm glad we caught that sunset. I'd love to see how those pictures come out." He whistled at Pepper. "I guess I'll be heading in now. Come on, boy. Time to go home."

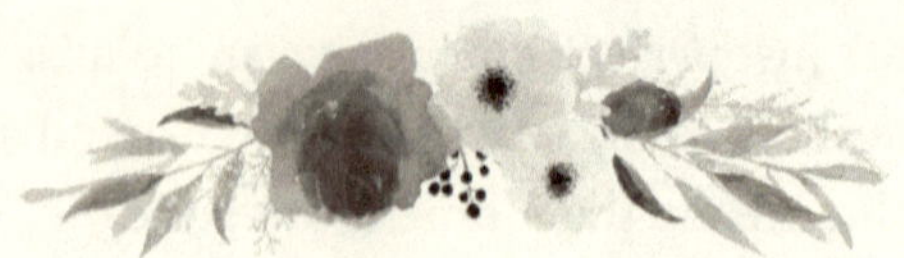

9

"What do you think of this one?" Beth Spencer pointed at the picture of a bouquet full of buttercups and peonies in the large album. She looked up appealingly into the eyes of her groom, Robert.

Jo-Ann leaned in. "Remember, anything you see can be customized. If there's a flower you'd rather replace, we can do that. And don't forget this handy little guide right here that arranges flowers by color."

Beth had been ooh-ing and aah-ing over the flower albums for well over an hour now. Jo-Ann and I could see what she could not. Her patient groom was beginning to lose patience. We both felt for him. Most grooms left choosing the flowers entirely up to their brides. Mothers or bridesmaids came into the shop with them and the grooms would forgo the hours of torture of deciding whether baby's breath or lily of the valley would better match their dress.

From the moment they'd arrived Robert doted on his new bride, calling her baby doll and listening patiently to her every requirement.

I bit my lip. This client would be difficult to please come

wedding day. Jo-Ann scribbled notes in her notebook about attending to various details. I knew she was thinking the same thing.

It had been a while since Robert had said anything. He'd given up, perhaps, after several versions of, "Whatever you want is what we should get, baby doll." And trying to guess what pleased his new bride. There was a reason grooms didn't come to these events. They could be tough on a romance—a couple's first sign of cracks in the marital foundation.

He stood and stepped away from the table. He made a signal to Jo-Ann, who was busy leafing through the photo album with Beth.

I took the cue and stood beside him. "I don't care what it costs," he whispered. "I don't care what color the flowers are, how big or how small the bouquets. I just want Beth to be happy. Is there anything you think you could suggest to her that would get us out of here before five o'clock? At this point, money is no object."

I smiled. I had just the idea. "How about purple calla lilies? I flipped to a page of the album with pictures of the stunning bouquets that Jo-Ann had made for the mayor's daughter's wedding two years previous. I'd seen them while flipping through the pictures trying to get acquainted with Jo-Ann's clientele.

Understanding sparked in Jo-Ann's eyes. "Beth, what do you think of these? We did these arrangements for Alexandra Bainbridge. They're a bold choice."

"Oooh. They're gorgeous. But there's baby's breath." She looked up at Jo-Ann with a frown.

"No problem. She wanted baby's breath. Personally, I think the calla lilies are far more classic all on their own. Like this." She flipped to a second photo.

I dashed to the refrigerator and snatched a couple of white and mauve roses and paired them with a purple and white calla lily and brought it back to the table. "And for the bridesmaid's bouquets, you could do something like this. You'll have to use your imagination just a little bit. There would be more of these in a round bouquet. But this is the kind of look you'd get."

"Oh, it's beautiful. I love it." She frowned again. "What about the price?"

Robert swooped in. "Price doesn't matter, baby. If it's what you love, it's what we'll have."

She smiled, tentatively. "But do *you* love it?"

"I do. The uh ..."

"Calla lily," I supplied.

"Right. Paired with the roses? It's perfect."

"I knew it was a good idea for you to come along," she said, and gave him a juicy kiss. "Well, we've made a decision then. Thank you ladies so much. I just know this is going to be the perfect wedding. Now all we have left to pick out is the cake."

Robert looked stricken.

"Hang in there," Jo-Ann whispered to him as she scooped up the photo albums and catalogues. "You're doing great."

She accompanied the couple to the door, said her good-byes and waved as they left the shop. She sighed as she joined me at the cash counter, where I was busy putting all the catalogues away into the cupboards they were kept in. "That wedding's going to be fun."

I winked at her. "You did great."

She shook her head. "That poor man. And people wonder why I never got married. They don't know what I see every day." She laughed, and her bosom shook.

I joined in. Jo-Ann's laughter was contagious.

"If you don't mind my asking, why *did* you never get married?" I'd wondered about that question often since I'd gotten to know her. She was such an easy-going person and told such fascinating stories about her life. She didn't seem like the type who would settle down with three cats to enjoy quiet evenings at home curled up with a book, yet that is what she claimed was her dream retirement.

"I was engaged once," she said. She looked at the clock. "We have a few minutes before the lunch hour. Do you want to nip down the street and get take-out from the Chinese restaurant? We can close the shop for fifteen minutes. I need some fresh air and to stretch my legs for a few minutes after that consultation. I'll tell you about it on the way."

"Sure." I'd packed a lunch, but her suggestion sounded good. I'd enjoyed getting to know Jo-Annm and I would miss her when our transition was complete.

She hung the "Back in Five Minutes" sign on the door, locked it, and we headed down Queen Street in the bright noonday sunshine.

My clothes stuck to me almost immediately in the August heat. "Nice day to be at the beach," I said.

Jo-Ann fanned herself. "No kidding. I didn't realize it was going to be so hot today. Maybe we should have ordered delivery." But her pace didn't slow as we made our way through the tourists gawking in shop windows and walking along the sidewalk, bikini-clad. "So, my engagement."

"Right." I hadn't wanted to prod her, but I was curious.

"You'll have to picture a much slenderer version of me. I was quite athletic in my day." Jo-Ann straightened up and sucked in her stomach, then let it all go with a chuckle. "Hard to imagine, isn't it?"

I laughed. "Not so hard."

"You're sweet," she said, touching my arm. "Look at that," she said, pointing at a sign in the window at Ricklands, one of Port Sandford's more swanky boutique gift stores. "Next week is sidewalk sale week."

"Oh right. I meant to mention it to Celia."

"She's coming back in town?"

"Next week. The last week before school starts. I always feel sad for Caleb when summer's over. Although I know he'll be busy with soccer practice and all his friends at school. I always love the summer."

"Maybe it's you you're sad for."

I nodded. "Maybe so. It'll be different this year, not being up there with them."

A slight trace of worry crossed her motherly face. "No regrets?"

"Of course not." I turned around. "We walked past the Chinese restaurant."

She scanned the line of shops. "You're right. We did. Too busy gabbing."

We walked into the restaurant, placed our order, and waited by the front desk, enjoying the air conditioning.

"He was training for the Olympics."

"Who?" I tried to identify who in the restaurant's lunch crowd she might be referring to.

"Sorry. I jump topics like a grasshopper in a cornfield. My high school sweetheart. He was a downhill skier. Just after graduation, he had a terrible accident. Broke his neck."

"Oh, that's awful."

Jo-Ann had a far-away expression. "It was a terrible time in my life. I stayed by his bedside every day for a year. But he was in a coma, and he never came out of it. His family finally decided to remove life support."

"I'm so sorry."

"You know how they say it's hard to compete with a first love." Jo-Ann smiled a sad smile. "It's just about impossible to compete with an Olympic hopeful first love who died tragically. It took me years to get over him and the way he died. By then, it seemed that marriage had passed me by."

Our order arrived, and we walked out into the heat again and along the street heading back toward the flower shop.

"How about you?" she asked. "Any high school sweethearts for you?"

A lump rose in my throat. "Nothing quite so tragic as your story. But I had a high school sweetheart. Frank. It just didn't work out."

Jo-Ann unlocked the door to the shop and took down the "Back in Five Minutes" sign. "Sounds like there's a lot more to *that* story. But I won't pry."

She spoke like someone who had every intention of doing just the opposite, yet she didn't. She picked up a magazine that had arrived in the mail that day and leafed through it. Nevertheless, I found myself thinking about Frank as I picked at my food with the cheap wooden chopsticks.

I met Frank my first day of high school. But it wasn't until grade eleven that we started dating. Later, he told me he knew from the first moment we met I would be his girl. I'm not sure that was really true for him. But it was for me. The moment I saw that sweet, crooked smile of his, the moment he brushed close to me and I smelled the smell of outdoors and soap on his clothes, it sent tingles and warmth all over me at the same time.

He stood behind me in a line outside the principal's office. Both of us had mix-ups in our schedules. I was scheduled to be in French class and Canadian Geography at the same time. He was trying to switch into the advanced math class.

He leaned toward me and elbowed me conspiratorially. "What are you in for?"

I looked up at him and blinked dumbly—at first because I had no idea what he was talking about. It had been years since we'd emigrated from Germany and my English was flawless, but I still missed some of its subtleties. I was often the last one to laugh at a joke, sometimes making me the butt of one. However, as I looked up into his face it wasn't my uncomprehension that left me speechless. Tender brown eyes met mine. And that smile ... I was smitten. I can't remember what I finally said in return. But that night, my head on my pillow, sleep the last thing on my mind, I kicked myself over it and rehearsed over and over what I would say the next time. If there ever was one.

And there was.

With him a sophomore and me a mere freshman, perhaps it was our age difference that prevented him from making a move that first year of school. But the first day of summer between my freshman and sophomore years, Frank took a job at the McPherson farm that bordered our property and made a detour to our front door.

He and I had been seeing each other more than a year when he asked me to dinner at his folks' place and told me he had a special announcement to make. I was so nervous getting ready for that evening I almost made myself sick. Frank's mother had made roast beef and her famous trifle for dessert, and I could barely touch a bite.

I'd worn the brand-new dress Mama had made me for the occasion. I was sure this was the night he would propose—the night I had dreamed of since that first day we'd met.

I was only halfway through the piece of trifle in the fancy parfait glass Mrs. Mayer had served me when Frank smiled that shy, crooked smile of his, pushed back from the table, and cleared his throat.

My stomach did a flip.

He reached for my hand but looked steadily at his parents. "I wanted you all to be here," he said, "when I told you the good news."

Mrs. Mayer beamed at her son, and I suddenly had the feeling I was left out again—like those jokes that went over my head.

"I'm going to attend Queen's University in the fall to study engineering."

Mr. Mayer stood, shook Frank's hand and pulled him in for a hug and a slap on the back. "So very proud of you, son."

Mrs. Mayer, her eyes now moist, continued beaming.

The room fell quiet. Frank looked at me. "Adele? You haven't said anything. What do you think? It's great news, isn't it? You know I've always dreamed of getting into Queen's."

Did I? Had we ever talked about it? Sure, he'd mentioned an interest in engineering, but four years at university? I forced a smile. "It's wonderful. I'm just ... so happy for you." I stood, hugged him awkwardly, and kissed his cheek. "It's just wonderful."

The room fell quiet again. Mrs. Mayer was seated across from me once more. "And what about you, dear? What do you intend to do after graduation?"

Heat rose in my cheeks. I sunk back into my chair. Five minutes earlier, I would have known exactly how to answer that question. *Why, marry your son, Mrs. Mayer. Be his wife, and eventually, the mother of his children. Frank will keep his job at the drug store and before long, we'll buy a cute little two-bedroom bungalow. I'll convert the spare bedroom into a studio and sell my works at the gallery in Ottawa. Your son is my forever love, and we're going to live happily ever after.*

But now, I had no answer at all. "I—I haven't decided."

Frank cleared his throat. "Adele's thinking about Ontario College of Art."

It was true. I'd thought about it. But it was a fleeting thought. Papa had no money to send me to art college—or any college.

"That's lovely, Adele. You'll have to bring over one of your paintings sometime. I'd love to see one." Mrs. Mayer lifted her napkin from the table and smoothed it over her lap again. "More trifle, anyone?"

Later that evening, Frank took off his jacket and put it over my shoulders as we strolled through the orchard behind his parents' property. All the apple trees were in bloom and only a few of the blossoms had succumbed to the spring wind and lay scattered on the path before us.

His parents, if they were watching—and I suspected they were—would have thought we were out for our usual meandering stroll. I suppose Frank thought the same thing. Only I knew differently.

"*Are* you happy for me?" Frank slowed his pace and bent to look at my face. And I was grateful the sun had set, and twilight's blue hue pervaded the orchard.

"Of course." I kept my eyes steadily on the path in front of me, where Mr. McPherson's tractor had made ruts between the rows of trees. "And I want you to be free to focus on your studies."

"What do you mean?" Frank tugged at my arm, as though he wanted me to stop and face him, but I kept the rhythm of my steps, my focus on the tractor treads. I had thought Frank was my one true love. I had thought our love would be my happily ever after. But I was wrong. This was wrong. I knew in the core of me that true love came easy—just like it did for Papa and Mama. Frank and I had hit a turn in the road and somehow we'd left the path of true love.

I stopped now, pulled his jacket from my shoulders, and shivered at the dampness that had settled on the farm. "Please take me home now."

When he dropped me off, I leaned over and kissed him on the cheek for the second time that evening. We said goodbye. For the last time.

Jo-Ann closed the magazine, stood and broke her chopsticks in half, then tucked the pieces inside her take-out container. She looked at my half-eaten food and touched my hand. "Aw, sweetie. Are you okay?"

I smiled. "Eyes bigger than my stomach, I guess." I wrapped up the container and popped it in the refrigerator. "Maybe I'll take it home for supper." Maybe then I wouldn't be so distracted. But how likely was that, when my barely-begun letter to Alfie waited for me on my desk?

10

———

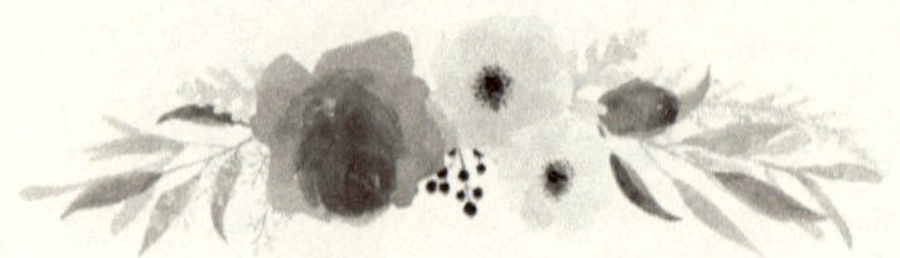

That evening, I built a fire in the fireplace to ward off the evening chill and sat down to write the letter to Alfie. However, two hours later I'd succeeded in writing just two words, "Dear Alfie."

I'd decided on the drive home that I needed to establish the right tone in the letter. I needed to put the past and its distractions behind me. My new life was here in Port Sandford. I was a business owner with new responsibilities, and it was time to move on. Alfie's questions deserved answers, and I didn't want to deny him knowing about Celia and his grandson. I needed to answer those questions—and nothing more. Once this letter was in the mail, I'd be able to put to rest the distracting thoughts and awakened memories.

However, I hadn't counted on how much being at the shop would remind me of the early days of our romance. After he walked out the door of the shop that day, I'd been flattered. But I thought that was the last I'd see of him. I told Margie I thought he was a big flirt.

"So, what are you going to do about it?" Margie smirked as

she looked at me standing there, the blush still left on my cheeks.

"Do about it? What do you mean? What could I do about it?"

"Call him up, go on a date ... that's what people do, you know."

I scowled at her. "Even if I wanted to—which I don't—and I could hide it from Mama—which I couldn't—all I know about him is his first name."

"Not true." From across the counter, she held up one of the flower cards. One of the ones that said, "Missing You" across the top. Down below, in blue ball-point were the words, *Alfie Hanson. Call me.* And a phone number.

My mouth fell open. "When did he do that?"

"Probably while you were getting the arrangement ready." She raised an eyebrow. "Sly one."

I shook my head. "Well, I can't call it."

Margie put a hand on her hip. "Why not? Lord knows you need a love life!"

I rolled my eyes. "Call a strange man's phone number? Are you kidding?" I surveyed the counter. Tidy. "Shouldn't we be getting back to wedding flowers?"

"He's not strange. You met him. He introduced himself." She smirked again. "And he's handsome."

"Those are not the only qualifications a man needs, you know."

Margie shrugged. "Works for me." She beckoned me to follow her to the back room. I was hoping the change of scenery would mean a change of topic. But she resumed her perch on the stool, picked up her shears, and started up again. "You know, your Mama doesn't need to know a thing about it."

I ignored that last comment. "He's got to be at least five years older than me."

"So that would make him what? Twenty-five? You're right. He's practically ancient."

I stood to bring a fresh supply of roses from the refrigerator.

"You told him your name," Margie said.

I flushed. "Yes, well, it was a moment of weakness."

"A moment of sanity, you mean." She sighed. "Adele, you're twenty years old, and your life consists of work and sleep. For heaven's sake, live a little."

"Fine. Give me the card." I reached across the table and took the card with Alfie Hanson's number. I slid it into my apron pocket.

"Don't put it there. You'll forget it. Get up and go put it in your handbag." Margie paused in her work and watched as I pushed away from the worktable, found my purse, and deposited the card inside it.

"Happy now?" I said.

"It's *your* happiness I'm concerned about," Margie said, and snipped decisively at a rose stem.

After that, thank goodness, the conversation turned to other topics. Sophie Beaulieu and her wedding, which both of us would attend—Sophie having been a classmate of mine and her mother a good friend of Margie's. And the weather, which had turned suddenly warm just in time for the wedding. Then there was the usual small-town gossip of Point-du-Fleuve, never in short supply, and regarding which Margie was always well-informed.

While Margie chattered on, my mind wandered often to Alfie Hanson. Each time it did, I forced it back to the moment. It had been lovely to feel the attention of a handsome stranger, but that's all it was, and I couldn't afford to be distracted by his advances. My paycheck wasn't huge, but by living frugally, I'd been able to save quite a bit aside. If I stayed my course, I'd be secure and self-sufficient. I would take care of myself. The next time I excused myself to the restroom, I pulled the card from my purse and threw it in the garbage.

However, that hadn't been the end of it either. Because four weeks later, while Margie and I were chatting over tea, Alfie swung open the door of the flower shop and took off his cap. "Afternoon, ladies!"

He strode to the counter and—right in front of Margie—handed me a bouquet of sweetheart roses he'd bought somewhere else.

"I figured I needed to take matters into my own hands," he said. "You were never going to call me, were you, Adele?"

I blushed—seemingly the only response I was capable of in the presence of this man.

He had arrived not long before closing time. "Have any plans tonight? I thought I'd take you out right now and do away with any chance you'd forget about me again."

As though I could have. The memory of those eyes and that smile had stayed vividly fresh every day of the month since his first visit to the shop.

I glanced at Margie, sure she had some part in this ambush, but she shrugged and raised both hands in a plea of innocence. After which she made her way to the back room in a show of giving us privacy, although she and I both knew she'd be watching in the mirror and straining for every word.

"I hear there's a nice little restaurant in Haverville. I'd be real pleased if you'd do me the honor of joining me for dinner there."

I glanced over my shoulder, aware that Margie would scold me for what I was about to say. "I can't. You're ... a stranger."

"But I'm not a stranger." Alfie smiled, a twinkle in those gray-blue eyes. "I introduced myself. You have my telephone number. And you've known me four whole weeks."

I laughed.

"And that's just what I want to do this evening—get to know

you better." Alfie leaned over the counter. His eyes never left mine.

I broke away from his gaze. "I'm sorry. I just can't."

He was quiet a moment. He put a hand on mine and nodded. "Okay. It's okay, Adele. I understand. Goodbye then."

The shop door jangled and Margie ran from the back room as quickly as her ample frame allowed.

"What just happened?"

I busied myself re-tying my apron. "He left."

"I know he left, but why?"

I shrugged. "He's a stranger, Margie. You don't really think I should take him up on his offer."

Margie sighed, placed a hand on my back and rubbed it softly.

I stared at the door. I knew I'd done the right thing. Yet something nagged uncomfortably at me. What if I'd just let true love walk out the door? It was rare, yes. But it did happen sometimes—like with Papa and Mama. What if the stranger I'd just rejected really was *the one*?

I put the pen down. Staring at the flowered stationery wasn't conjuring up any more words. I strode to the counter, plugged in the kettle, and found a tea bag.

A lump rose in my throat. How wrong I'd been to think he was the one. I had been so naive then, believing Alfie and I could find the kind of true love my Papa and Mama had shared. It was wrong from the start. But it hadn't seemed that way.

In four more weeks—when he received his paycheck, as I discovered later—Alfie walked through the door again. I'd been counting the days on the calendar on my checkbook. I didn't have any reason to think he'd return. But I hoped.

Each time the bell over the door rang, I dashed to the front of the shop.

"Dear girl, what is wrong with you?" Margie half-scolded. "Too much caffeine?"

We were waist-high in funeral flowers. David Dupré, a flamboyant concert pianist and favorite music teacher who'd made Point-du-Fleuve his home in his later years had died and it seemed everyone in town had ordered arrangements to be sent to the funeral home.

Finally, an hour before closing, Alfie appeared at the door.

He handed me a long-stemmed pink rose. Then looked over my shoulder toward the back room. "Where's your boss?"

"My boss? You mean Margie? She's in the back. We're up to our eyeballs in funeral flowers."

His shoulders slumped a little. "So I guess she won't let you leave for a little while?"

I motioned to the clutter in the store. Even the retail space was filled with flower arrangements ready to send to the funeral home. "I'm afraid not. Just take a look. These are the ones we've already finished today." I sighed. "Our delivery man called in sick today. What did you have in mind?"

"I was going to ask you if you'd join me in a walk by the river. I figured you didn't like the idea of going to Haverville in the evening with a stranger, but you couldn't object to walking with me in plain daylight here in town. And I'd have you back before closing, if your boss—"

"Margie."

"Right. Margie—if she could spare you."

Whoever Alfie Hanson was, he was persistent. And he was definitely scoring points with me for his ingenuity. He was right. An afternoon walk by the river did sound lovely—and harmless enough.

Alfie was surveying the flower arrangements. "I'll tell you

what. Why don't I stick around a while and help you? Starting with these flower arrangements. Could I deliver them for you?"

At that, Margie came running out from the back room. "Are you serious? You'd do that?"

Alfie grinned. "Sure. Why not? As long as when I'm finished, you'll let me lend a hand here as well."

Margie looked at me then back to Alfie. "I'm sure we can find something for you to do. Just wait a moment while I draw you a map for directions to the funeral home and grab the keys for the van."

After we helped Alfie load all the flowers into the van and he drove off, Margie and I returned to our work in the back room. "Are you sure that was a good idea?"

"What? Letting Alfie handle all those deliveries? It's a great idea." Margie picked up where she left off with an all-white arrangement featuring fragrant lilies. Mine was a smaller arrangement with some of the same flowers.

"You just let a stranger drive off with your delivery van and several hundred dollars' worth of flowers."

She shook her head and laughed. "You think he's going to set up a booth somewhere and hawk my bouquets? The man is doing something nice out of the goodness of his heart." She looked up. "And because he's trying to win your affections."

I smiled. "Seems like he already has yours."

"You're right about that. I have a good feeling about that man. I have since the day he walked in here."

I raised an eyebrow at her. "You never said so to me."

She cocked her head to one side. "Would you have listened?"

She was right. I wouldn't have.

"I'm telling you, you need to lighten up a little and learn to trust more. You keep calling him a stranger, but you don't give him a chance to be anything else."

Half an hour later, when Alfie walked back into the store,

Margie gave me a look that had *I told you so* written all over it. He headed straight for the back room and rolled up his sleeves. "What can I do?"

Margie waved her clippers around, indicating the broom in the corner. "We've been so busy there's been no chance to clean up all these stems and leaves on the floor. You can take the broom there and sweep them into piles. There are garbage bags in that cupboard over there." She waved the clippers again. "You can put all the clippings into one of those and hang it over the back of the chair in the corner so we can clean as we go from here on out."

"Yes, ma'am." Alfie grabbed the broom and set to work.

While he worked, Margie plied him with questions. "So, Alfie, we've been wondering, what brings you to Point-du-Fleuve?"

I shot a look at her. *We've* been wondering?

She ignored me.

He swept briskly, gathering all the cuttings into piles on the floor. "Well, it's *through* town actually. I live on the army base at Camp Petawawa, and my mom lives near Otter Lake. I drive home when I can to see her and take her a little money. And I have friends out that way as well."

Margie looked meaningfully in my direction. I was glad I wasn't beside her because I was sure she would have nudged me.

"You're enlisted then?" Margie asked.

"Eighteen more months." Alfie bent and scooped all the clippings into the garbage bag.

I looked up. "And then what?"

He shrugged and his eyes met mine. "Might be time to think about settling down."

I blushed again.

Alfie picked up the broom. "How many more arrangements do you need to do today?

Margie reached for the pair of glasses that hung on a chain around her neck and consulted the master order list. "What do you know—just one more. Adele, you finish up with the arrangement you're working on and tidy up. Alfie, if you wouldn't mind, give the floor in the front a quick going-over with that broom. And then you two can head out. I'll finish up this last one."

I finished placing the last few stems, tidied up my workspace, and tiptoed to the doorway to watch as Alfie swept. Who was this man who was pursuing me? What kind of man would give up his plans for a date in favor of an afternoon of errands and keeping shop with a woman who'd twice rejected him and her nosy boss? Maybe Margie was right. I certainly wasn't going to find out if I didn't give him a chance.

I stepped into the room, and Alfie looked up. "So, what are your plans now?"

He laughed. "Isn't that my line?"

"Is it too late for that walk by the river?"

His eyebrows raised. "Really?"

The walk by the river was beautiful in the early evening light. I didn't stay long that time. I didn't want Mama to worry about me and I wasn't yet ready to tell her anything about Alfie. But our after-work walks became a regular event. Whenever he was granted leave after he received his paycheck, he'd drive through Point-du-Fleuve and stop in at the flower shop. I marked my calendar for his visits all that spring and into the summer and fall. In winter, he came less frequently, whenever the weather allowed. Visits came more regularly the following spring, marked by a change of venue: dinner at my house with Mama and Papa. On one of those visits, Alfie Hanson got down on one knee after dinner and—right there in our living room— he proposed.

The kettle had long ago boiled. I poured water over the tea bag and carried the mug back to the desk.

I read Alfie's letter one more time. How difficult did it need to be to write a letter? I could do this. I lifted my pen and wrote in a fluid motion, not allowing myself to stop and overthink the words.

Dear Alfie,

What a surprise to hear from you after all these years. I'm glad to hear you are doing well. I appreciate your apology, but it really isn't necessary. Although I can't pretend I understand exactly what happened between us, I forgave you long ago.

Celia is well and happy. She took a program in Early Childhood Education in Toronto, and while she was there, she met a wonderful man named Jeff. She and Jeff had some difficulty getting pregnant. They finally had a miracle baby boy they named Caleb. He is seven years old now. He plays soccer during the school year and comes every summer to the cottage. He is a delightful, clever boy, although I am naturally biased in saying so.

We did move out of the old house in Point-du-Fleuve, so you were right to write me at the cottage. We moved to another, smaller home in town, but I am preparing to sell it now too. I have appreciated the cottage over the years, and now I'll get to enjoy it all the time when I move here permanently.

I'm happy to know that you have found what gives you fulfillment. I wish you all the best.

Adele

I folded the letter, put it in an envelope, affixed a stamp, and tucked it in my purse. I'd mail it in the morning from the mailbox on the street near the flower shop.

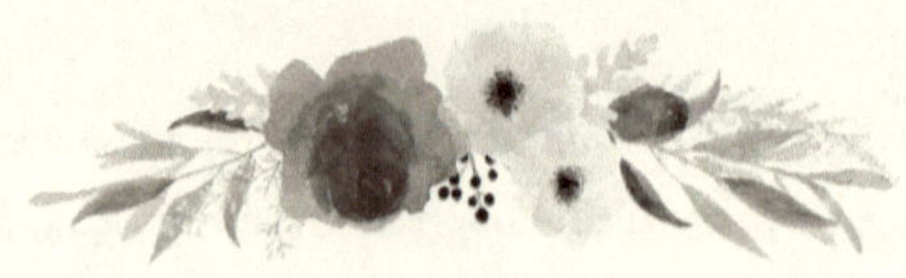

11

*V*ictor Guthier met me on the front lawn. He raised his hand to shield against the morning sun. "How old's the roof?"

I frowned. The roof had always been on my list of things to fix. It had held up well, but shingles were turning up all over the place. Even I could see it clearly needed fixing. "I'm afraid it hasn't been replaced for twenty years."

The house had been good to us. Few things had broken down or worn out while we'd lived there. However, that also meant not much renovation had been done over the years. I just never had the budget for it.

He clicked the end of his pen and wrote something on a checklist in his fancy leather-bound clipboard. "Okay, well let's go on inside and have a look then, shall we?"

As we walked to the side door, I congratulated myself that at least all the gardens around the house still looked beautiful on the cool September morning. We stepped inside and up the short flight of stairs into the kitchen. I bit my lip as he made notes again on the clipboard.

"That wallpaper …"

"I know. Needs to go." Nothing a good coat of paint and a lot of elbow grease wouldn't fix, I was sure, but I hadn't really bargained on spending so much time in Point-du-Fleuve before heading back again to the shop. Hiring someone to do the work was out of the question, especially if the roof needed fixing.

"And the dark-wood cabinets." He walked closer to inspect them. "Maybe a nice coat of white paint?"

The side door opened, and in walked my baby sister, Hannah. "How's it going?" she mouthed before slipping off her shoes and placing them on the floormat at the door. She tiptoed up the stairs to join me where I braced for the real estate agent's assessment.

"So far, the roof, the kitchen cabinets, and the wallpaper."

She gave my arm a squeeze and stood close. "Right, but we knew all that." She smiled at the real estate agent and extended her hand. "Hannah Derby, Adele's sister."

He shook it. "Nice to meet you. Victor Guthier. Call me Vic." He smiled at me. "Okay, where to next?"

"The bathrooms, I guess. And the bedrooms." I swallowed hard. The bathroom fixtures were pretty dated. What would he say about them?

We walked around from room to room, Victor making his notes all the while. Hannah, gutsier than i was, walked up and peered over his shoulder at his notes.

"Is he writing anything good?" I whispered.

"Who knows. His handwriting's illegible."

When we'd walked over the entire property, including the toolshed in the backyard where I kept my lawnmower and garden tools, Victor suggested we go inside to the kitchen table to discuss what it would take to sell my house.

As we approached the door, Celia's Camry pulled up. She parked in front of the house, behind Hannah's car, the small driveway having reached capacity with my car and the real estate agent's.

"Sorry. Had to get Caleb off to school, and then Jeff needed help finding some files in the office. What did I miss?"

"We're just about to hear the assessment, so you're just in time." I squeezed her hand. I'd been in town a couple of days, so they'd already had me for dinner the evening before.

We sat down, and the agent explained all the work I'd need to do to get the house ready for sale. After he left, I looked at Hannah and Celia, feeling like a boat adrift on the lake, no wind behind me anymore.

Hannah was the first to speak. "Look, there wasn't really anything on that list that took us by surprise. We can't do much about the fact that the house has just two bedrooms. But the furnace and windows are all in good shape. You heard him say that, right?"

I nodded.

She looked up at the ceilings and the walls. "What this place mostly needs is love."

Celia squeezed my hand. "This place had a lot of love."

Hannah folded us both in a hug. "Aw. Of course it did, sweetie. It's just that now it needs a little more." She rolled up her sleeves. "I can take some time off work."

"And I'm available, once Caleb's off to school," Celia said.

Hannah smiled, hopefully. "Let's get busy."

"Some of this is going to take money. The roof..."

Hannah nodded. "Okay, your first job is getting a quote on that."

"And paint." I scowled at the kitchen cabinets and walls.

"I'm pretty sure we've got a bunch of leftover paint from when we renovated the great room, Mom. Maybe enough to finish the kitchen. You liked that color, right?" She looked at the cabinets. "Jeff might know someone who could help us out with those kitchen cabinets. Let me work on that."

"If you can get the name of the paint, Celia, we can see if we can match it at the paint store and get a price. You may as well do the bedrooms the same color, like the agent said."

I hugged both of them. "Thank you. I don't know what I'd do without either of you."

"The real estate agent said to leave some of the furniture in place so the house looks lived in, but there's plenty we can pack up too, while we're at it."

I sighed. "The attic." I looked at Hannah. "You know there's a bunch of stuff up there that came from Mom's place after she died and hasn't even been opened since—not even when we moved the last time."

Hannah smiled. "Well, we've got our work cut out for us."

By the next morning, roofers were at work on the roof, Jeff and a friend of his who was between construction jobs were ripping out the kitchen cabinets. They planned to replace them with newer ones they'd salvaged for a very reasonable price. Celia and I were at work peeling wallpaper from one of the bedrooms, and Hannah had been upstairs in the attic assessing the extent of the job up there. She came into the room carrying a stack of old photographs. She sat down on the bed and put the stack beside her. "Look at these."

Celia sat on the bed.

"I'd forgotten how beautiful she was," Celia said.

I lowered myself beside her and rubbed her back. She had been so young when Mama—her Nana—died.

"She *was* beautiful," Hannah breathed.

Mama had a quiet grace that commanded respect. Her values and manners were from the "old country," but she had a way of making you know that was a good thing.

I touched the glass of the picture frame. "I miss her."

We continued to flip through the photographs, most of which weren't framed, like the first one. "Look at this one." Hannah held up a photograph that perfectly captured the way Mama always looked at Papa—a combination of affection and a certain knowing. As though she understood everything about him. How that was possible, I'd never understand. It was something that had eluded me in all my relationships with men. It was that look that first convinced me of the existence of true love. One day stood out and still lived bright in my memory. Papa had been gone a long time. I don't remember exactly how long or even exactly why. "Business" was all Mama told me at the time.

I missed Papa that summer.

It wasn't as though Mama couldn't handle the household all on her own. That summer she did laundry, kept house, weeded the garden, and mowed the lawn. And she put up dozens of jars of peach preserves and green beans and tomatoes. I know because I helped with most of them. Mama said I was big enough. Unlike Hannah who had to stay in her playpen with her dollies, safe from scalding water and steaming stovetops.

But I missed the feeling of him in the house. His tucking me into bed at night. His kiss and the smell of his Aqua Velva when he left for work in the morning.

Maybe that's why I remember so clearly the day he came back, down to the date on the calendar: August 28, 1957. I can still see the look on his face as he handed Mama a big bouquet and swept her off her feet. They danced in the pink light of the sunset that streamed through the kitchen window, illuminating for a heartbeat the wet trail from the tear that snuck down Mama's cheek. He whispered in her ear and winked at me over her shoulder.

I watched them, my head resting on my hands as I sat backwards on the big kitchen chair the way Mama disliked because it wasn't *damenhaft*—ladylike.

I could have watched them like that forever. And I knew then. Knew like you know your name or where your hand is in the dark. I knew that what I was watching between Papa and Mama, bathed in the glow of that Laurentian sunset, was the way love was supposed to be. True love that came easily—naturally. Forever love. A true happily-ever-after story. And I knew I would never want anything less.

"Look, Adele, here's one of you and me." Hannah passed me the photograph. It was black and white—the kind with the white edges all around, and she and I were all dressed up in dresses. Although it wasn't possible to tell from the photograph, I remembered clearly that the dresses were pink. Mama had sewn them. Although Hannah was six years my junior, we were dressed like twins—something Mama was fond of doing. But I never minded. I adored my little sister. "Look at your little dimples. Where did you find all these?"

"Mama's big old trunk is up in your attic. There's a bunch of old things in it. You didn't know?"

I shook my head. "After Mama died, I didn't have the heart to look through it. I was too sad. It was just too much. Now that you mention it, I guess I knew it was up there—"

"With a whole lot of other things piled on top of it."

I shrugged. "Like I said, I just didn't have the heart."

Hannah stared down at the pile of black and white memories. "Do you mind if I take a few of these photographs? I have so few of her."

I gave her arm a little squeeze. "Of course. Take whatever you want. You didn't need to ask. Heaven knows I won't have room for all of it at the cottage, anyway. And if you want the old trunk—"

"Really?" Hannah's smile spread from ear to ear. She still had that cute little dimple.

"Of course."

Hannah started sifting through the pile again. I stopped her, briefly. "But would you mind leaving me the one of her and Papa together?"

"Of course. Why don't I swap it out for this other one in the frame? They're the same size." She continued sorting the pile, moving through the years. My sixteenth birthday, then Hannah's. She stopped and looked up at me. "What do you want me to do with this?" It was a picture of me and Alfie on our wedding day. I stared at it. There was the look. I'd had it too. The same look my mother had in the photo of her and Papa. But how was that possible?

"Wow, do you ever look like Mama in this picture. I never noticed before."

Celia peered over her shoulder, saw the image of her father, and looked away. "You could burn it."

I searched Hannah's eyes. Did she still remember that day as I did?

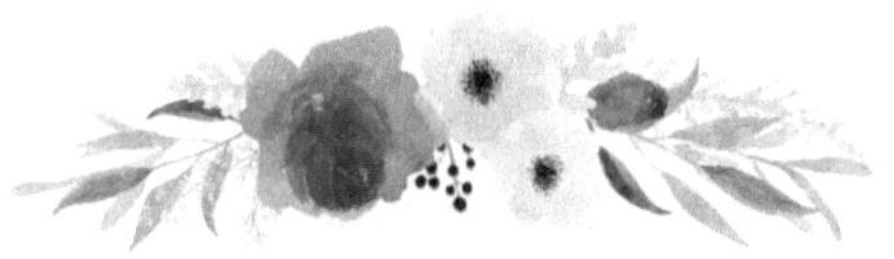

12

The ceremony had been perfect. The flower girl froze halfway to the altar at the sight of so many people with their eyes on her, the ring bearer tripped three times on his way up the petal-strewn aisle, causing everyone to laugh—and the ring bearer to cry. And, of course, Margie outdid herself with the wedding flowers. She had her sisters come in and help her with the bouquets and centerpieces so I could focus on the other arrangements and so I would see everything for the first time on my special day. And she refused to take any money from Papa and Mama for any of them. With the exception of the flowers, the wedding wasn't lavish, by anyone's standards. But it was just perfect as far as I was concerned. We held the service at the one and only Protestant church in town and took our photos on the front steps and lawn of the church. I couldn't have been happier if it had been Buckingham Palace.

After the photos, we moved back inside to the church basement for a meal catered by the ladies auxiliary. For a small wedding, we had a lot of people at the head table. Mama wanted me to choose just one friend to be maid of honor with no additional bridesmaids. I knew right away that my little sister Hannah would be my maid of honor. But that left me with no way to honor Margie and all she'd done to help Alfie and me get together. And there was Candice, my best friend from high school in whose wedding I'd stood as maid of honor. Alfie was similarly torn. He had three best friends from his detachment in the army and couldn't imagine not asking all three of them to be a part of our special day. So in the end, we decided on three bridesmaids and three groomsmen. While she was sewing their dresses, Mama made a show of grumbling about all the work, but she was as giddy as I was about anything to do with my wedding plans.

She had liked Alfie immediately, and although she joined Papa's well-wishes to Alfie during the wedding toasts and welcomed him into the family, it was strictly a formality. Alfie had been made to feel like family from the first dinner he sat at our table.

After Papa's toast, Alfie's friend Patty—short for Patterson, since no one called him by his first name apparently—stood to make his speech.

He raised his glass and shook his head. "Alfie, my man. I've been standing here all day thinking one thing: I can't believe you're tying the knot. You're the last guy I'd have ever expected to go out and get yourself the old ball and chain." There was a bit of laughter from the table where some of Alfie's other friends sat. Patty looked up and raised his glass toward his pals. "Am I right? But one look at your bride and anyone with half a brain can see why you gave up bachelorhood. I wish you both all the best." He walked over and caught Alfie in a hug before he took his seat again.

Alfie returned to his place beside me and pulled in his chair. He cast a glance in my direction. "You okay? You look a little ill."

I did feel ill. What did Patty mean, *you're the last guy I ever expected it of?* But before I had a chance to make a comment,

Adrien Caron pushed his chair out from the table noisily and stood unsteadily to his feet. "Alfie. What can I say? You're married. It's going to take some getting used to. I can hardly believe it. Like Patty said, out of all of us, you're the last one I expected to see getting hitched. But I couldn't be happier for ya, man. Adele, you hang on to that guy. He's quite the catch—or so the ladies tell me." He raised his glass high. "To Alfie."

The seventy-five or so guests all raised their glasses in response.

He sat down, then jumped back up again. "And Adele. To Alfie and Adele."

The guests toasted again. I began to feel flushed.

Finally, Alfie's best man Thomas stood. He smiled at me and at Alfie and lifted his glass. I took a deep breath. "Alfie, I know that on this day, I'm your best man, but you have been the best friend to me over the years. I know I don't say it enough, but it's true. You've been there for me, through thick and thin. You have supported me through all the messes I've gotten myself into and you've never, ever let me down. I guess I was as surprised as anyone else that you're settling down, but you couldn't have found yourself a more beautiful bride. You take good care of her."

With that, the speeches were finished. I couldn't have been more relieved. I was practically sweating. I needed to get out to the ladies' room or step outside for a little air. Hannah leaned over and whispered in my ear. "Are you okay?"

I shook my head.

"Come with me." She tapped Alfie on his shoulder, and he turned and looked at her. "I just need to steal your bride for two minutes—it's a sister thing."

"Bring her back soon. I'm about to take my wife out on that dance floor and show her some moves."

"We'll be right back." She tugged on my arm. "Won't we Adele?"

I nodded and fought back a wave of nausea as I followed Hannah to the restroom at the back of the hall. Once inside the door, she sat down on the countertop at the sink and gave me her undivided attention. "Okay, what is going on?"

I paced, unable to control my nervous energy. "I don't know. I ... did you hear those speeches?"

"What? You mean Alfie's groomsmen?" Hannah tracked me as I walked back and forth.

I nodded. "Every single one of them said they couldn't believe Alfie was getting married."

"Yeah sure, but—"

"Hannah, what have I done?" I avoided the sight of myself in the mirror, all dolled up in my wedding dress, the picture of the hopeful bride. My own image mocking me.

Hannah jumped down from the counter. "Whoa, whoa, whoa." She grabbed me by both shoulders. "Slow down and make some sense. What are you talking about, 'what have you done?' You've married the love of your life. That's what you've done." Her voice was Mama's, soft and soothing.

The image of Frank leapt before my eyes. At one time, I had thought he was the love of my life. And look how that turned out. Had I been wrong again?

"Every one of them said it, Hannah—"

"Yeah, so, every one of them is a jerk. You didn't marry *them*. You married him."

"I know but—"

"They're his army buddies, Adele, they're not from the country club. They meant well. Their hearts were in the right place. They also said he was a good friend. Always stood by them. Did a smart thing by choosing you. Did you hear any of *that*?" She still held me by the shoulders, her blue eyes pleading with me as much as her words.

"But—"

She smoothed my hair. "Look. It's been an emotional day. The most emotional day of your life. You're married, big sister."

I fought the anxiety that rose in my chest. "I know. I know."

She continued to smooth my hair. "And you found a good man. Mama loves him. Papa loves him. You heard *their* speech, right?"

I nodded.

"And Margie loves him. So do I. He's a good man, Adele. And you've made a good decision marrying him. Trust it."

I gazed into her eyes again. I nodded.

She glanced toward the door. "You ready to go out?"

"I think so."

"Take a deep breath."

I did as I was told and felt my breath catch before I let it out all the way. I did feel better. What would I do without her? "*I'm supposed to be the big sister, full of sage advice.*"

Hannah put her arms around me. "Yeah, well. You'll have your moment when I get married. Don't worry."

I hugged her tight. "It won't be the same. We won't be under the same roof anymore."

Hannah squeezed back. "I know. I'm going to miss you ... but Mama said I can have your room."

I laughed and wiped away a tear. Hannah pushed me away. "Now go. Your handsome *husband* is waiting for his first dance."

I stared at the photograph in Hannah's hands. "I'll keep it," I said and looked away. "Just leave it in the pile of things to be sorted."

Celia looked at me sharply. "Really, Mom?"

"It's a memory, honey. I can't deny it happened." Nor could I deny the mystery of that look.

13

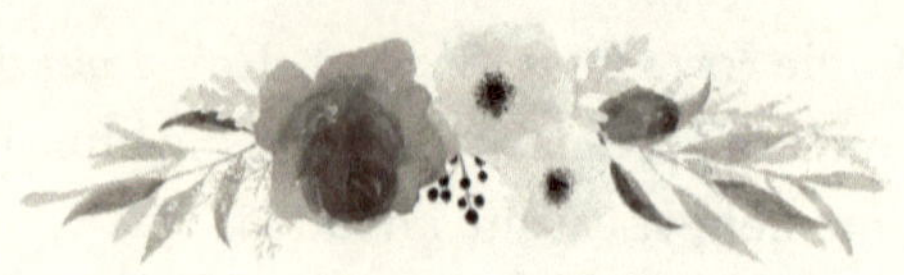

stared out at the lake. It had lost the lazy face it wore in the summer. In the month or more I'd been away, I'd missed the transition to the darker blue, colder face it assumed in October and November. In previous years, I'd have already begun to think about how to close things up for the winter. I smiled as I realized afresh that I would be enjoying this view all year long from now on.

The house in Point-du-Fleuve hadn't sold yet, but our cobbled-together team had done a lot of work in a short time—enough to satisfy the real estate agent and convince him to show the house to three families so far. Another interested family would be looking at it later today he said. In the meantime, I'd been anxious to get back to the shop and resume learning the business. I'd missed three weddings and as many funerals in September, and I felt I couldn't stay away a moment longer.

Today had been my first day back, and for the first time, things started to feel like mine instead of just Jo-Ann's. I was hoping to raise the subject of hanging some of my paintings there later this week.

I pulled on my sneakers and walked down to the beach. It wouldn't be long before snow piled up outside and it would be difficult to go out the back door to the shore every day. I wanted to take as many opportunities as I could to enjoy a walk near the water. And I had a destination in mind.

I wanted to update Jack on all that had been going on while I'd been away. And I'd had an idea. While painting two bedrooms and a kitchen, when I wasn't laughing at something Hannah said or talking with Celia, I'd had a lot of time to think about whatever it was that was going on between Jack and me. I figured we were putting too much pressure on ourselves by going out on formal dates or even walks together. What we needed was for things to feel familiar again—for us to pick up our friendship where it had left off and allow it to naturally bloom into something more. Or not.

I hoped to invite him to my place to have a good, old-fashioned games night, just like we used to have. I'd brought a whole new stack of games with me from the house at Point-du-Fleuve, and I planned to bake a pie with some of the berries I'd found in the freezer at the house.

Despite my plan, my stomach churned as I walked toward Jack's place. I still hadn't sorted out the feelings I had for him. Was my nervousness a result of excitement to see him, or because of anxiety over his feelings for me?

I reached his place, and before I could knock at the door, Pepper, ever the watchful guard dog, had sounded the alarm inside. I glanced up the hill through the woods but couldn't tell clearly whether Jack's car sat outside the house or not. Maybe he wasn't home.

Just when I was ready to turn away and head back to my cottage, Jack appeared at the door. He looked tired and his eyes were red. He smiled, although not with his usual enthusiasm, and opened the door.

"Well, hello, stranger." He gave me a hug. "How have you been?"

"Busy."

"Are you all moved in?" Jack led me to the kitchen table and motioned for me to sit while he started up the coffee pot. He seemed to move more slowly than normal.

"I'm not. I brought a load of things back—better dishes to replace the beat-up ones at the cottage, my winter clothes, some books, games, and old photographs. But I donated or threw out an awful lot of stuff, and Celia and Hannah even helped me organize a yard sale one weekend. There's still some furniture I'll likely sell online, but most of the time we spent trying to get the house ready to sell. Did you know that 1980s wallpaper patterns are not popular now?"

Jack humphed. "A lot of work, I'll bet."

I nodded. "More than I was prepared for." A photo album sat on the table. I flipped it open. Emma's smiling face looked up at me from some far-away place. Italy, perhaps, by the look of the scenery. "I see you've been looking at old photographs too."

Jack looked up from the kitchen sink, the light from the window over it highlighting his red eyes. "It's the anniversary today."

"Your wedding anniversary?"

He shook his head. "She died five years ago today."

I closed the photo album. "Oh, Jack. I'm so sorry. Really." I stood up. "Do you want me to leave you alone?"

"No, it's a good thing you stopped by. I've been worried about you. I was afraid you'd turned tail and weren't coming back. Thought maybe I'd scared you off."

I smiled and faltered for a reply. Jack's directness was forever throwing me off balance. "Of course not," I finally managed.

He shrugged. "The thought occurred to me. And I've spent

enough time alone with her memory. It's good to talk to someone."

I opened the photo album back up again. "This was a trip to Europe?"

"Mostly Italy." He brought the coffee cups to the table, along with cream for me. "It was her favorite place. Before we built this cottage, she tried to convince me to move there instead. She fell in love with a little town in Tuscany. She had a little villa picked out and had figured out how much it would cost for us to live there half the year and back here in Canada the other half."

"But you never did. Why not?" I looked at Emma's beaming face in each photographs as Jack turned the pages. She certainly looked happy and in her element. The way I felt when I painted.

Jack took a deep, slow breath and let it out again before he answered. "I didn't want to. It wasn't my favorite place, and I was too blind to see how happy it made her. I guess I was punishing myself by looking at these photos today." He shook his head. "I've spent a lot of time wondering, 'what if.'"

I put my hand on his to stop him flipping the pages. "You two were happy here ..."

"After a while. The whole time it was being built, and for a little while afterward, she didn't come out to look at the cottage. She stayed at the house in Toronto. I don't know if maybe she wasn't thinking she would leave me and go live in Tuscany without me."

I stared at Jack. "I never knew."

Jack smiled a wry smile. "I don't have to tell you the kinds of things that can go on within a marriage. You haven't talked much about what happened between you and your ex-husband, but we all have our stories of struggle. The preacher pronounces you man and wife at the wedding, but nobody hands you a manual for the life that starts the day after. What they don't tell you is a good marriage takes work. Hard work and lots of it."

I pondered his words. He was right. No one told you that.

I thought again about my parents and the photograph that captured their love so perfectly—the love I'd spent my whole marriage looking for and seeming never to find. And yet that second photograph of Alfie and me on our wedding day nagged at me. It was as though I had the pieces to two different puzzles and had been trying to put them together, not understanding why they wouldn't fit.

Jack took a sip of his coffee. "It's a testament to her character—not mine—that she came out to live here with me and learned to love it—and she learned to love me again. She was quite a woman. I didn't deserve her."

I took a sip of my coffee. I didn't know how to respond. She *was* quite a woman. But there was obviously much more to her —to them—I'd never realized. "No one would ever have known, looking at the two of you, that there was ever anything wrong. Your marriage seemed ... perfect." *Like Mama and Papa's.*

He smiled. "Well, I guess that's good to hear. But maybe it speaks more to our ability to fake it until we made it than anything else." He smiled sadly at Emma's image standing in the middle of a vineyard, holding up a glass of wine. "I wonder, you know?"

"Wonder what?" I searched his soft brown eyes.

"What it would have been like if I'd been the one to compromise. If I'd been the bigger man. If I'd agreed to go to Tuscany. She was so happy there. Maybe the bitter pill of disappointment over our marriage was the real cancer."

"Oh, Jack. Don't think that."

He shrugged. "How can I not? If she moved here and learned to love this cottage, couldn't I have moved to Tuscany and learned to love it there? Or what's to say we couldn't have built a smaller cottage on a less expensive piece of land somewhere else and lived here half the year and in Tuscany half the year, like she said."

"I'm sure Emma forgave you, Jack." I touched his hand.

He looked up at me, eyes moist, smiling sadly. "Yes, I think she did."

My walk back to my own cottage along the beach was slower. A storm was brewing over the lake and the sky had turned menacing, the water choppy and dark. I took my time anyway. It had been a lot to take in. I'd never seen Jack like that. I felt closer to him, somehow. And I hurt for him. To live all those years with regrets—I couldn't imagine. Or could I?

The warmth of the cottage greeted me, but five minutes after I'd arrived and hung up my coat, I felt the chill again. I built a fire in the fireplace and made a cup of tea, then spotted the pile of mail on the counter. I'd changed my mailing address at the post office, so mail was forwarding here from Point-du-Fleuve, meaning I now received more than just a stack of flyers and the local free paper. I rifled through it, throwing most of it in the trash until I came to another letter with the familiar handwriting.

Alfie had written me again.

I took the letter to the sofa in front of the fireplace and stared at it a moment before opening it. What more could he want to say to me after all these years? I ripped it open.

Dear Adele,

It was so good to see your letter in the mail. I held it for a long time just studying your handwriting. It was just good to know you'd received my letter and had taken the time to write me back. But I was a little afraid about what you might have to say. What if you'd decided not to forgive me? What if you had bad news about Celia?

I was so glad to hear she is happy. With a son. I'm sure she's a wonderful mother. She had the best example to follow.

Adele, I was a fool, all those years ago. It's real important to me that you know I've changed. I'm not the same man I was thirty years ago. I know it's hard to believe the word of a man who walked out on you. A man who did the things I did. In these last two years since my life has turned around, I've spent a lot of hours trying to make amends for all those things. Sounds stupid, I know, when I've only just now got in touch with you. But I didn't feel worthy even to write you a letter—not then.

But then Pastor Manuel told me there wasn't anything I could do to earn forgiveness. Not from God and not from you. He said I just had to accept it.

That was hard to take. A man wants to earn something—to do something. So, for a long time I've been working on just accepting that forgiveness. And forgiving myself.

I'm telling you all this so you'll know how much it meant to read that you've forgiven me. Kinda funny that I was working so hard for something you and God had already done.

And I'm telling you because, if it's all right, I'd like to keep writing to you. It was so good to hear from you. I've missed you, Adele. Aside from the Good Lord, you were the best thing that ever happened to me.

Alfie

14

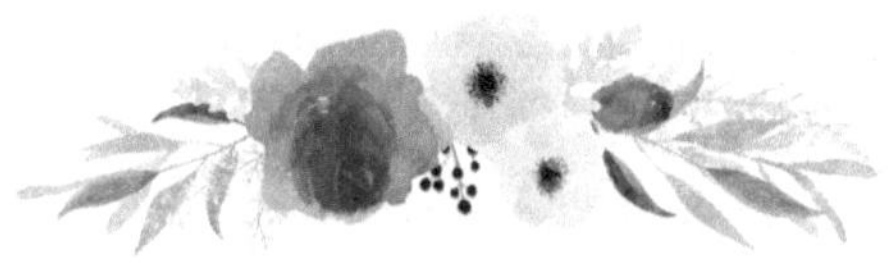

"Quartzy?"

Jack laughed. "It's a word, I promise you. It means, 'Resembling quartz'"

"Impressive." I counted the tiles. "That's 164 points to you." I stood to pour myself another cup of coffee. I held up the pot. "How about you?"

"Better not. It's getting late."

I'd never gotten around to inviting Jack for games night on the anniversary of Emma's death. It hadn't seemed appropriate. But the next time I saw him, I finally made my proposal. When he arrived, he built a fire in the fireplace to keep the November chill at bay, and we'd had chili for supper and one of my famous pies for dessert. We'd played a round or two of Canasta and now he was beating me at Scrabble.

I sat back down at the table, studying my collection of tiles. Two Ys, an M, an X, two Is and an A. I turned my attention from the dismal prospects and fired a question at Jack. "Do you think people can change? I mean like 180-degree kind of change?"

Jack placed four tiles on the board. J-A-Z-Z-Y. He sighed. "I didn't. Not in time. But yeah. I believe people can change. I think that's one thing that sets us apart from other animals. Our ability to learn from our mistakes. To change and grow."

I lowered my coffee mug. "You're quite the philosopher."

He shrugged. "You brought it up. What makes you ask?"

I shook my head. "Oh, an old friend got in touch. He says he's changed. I've been thinking a lot about it."

"So, do you believe he's changed?"

I set down two letters—an M and a Y around the A in Jack's JAZZY. "I'd like to think so."

"What makes you doubt him?"

"History, I suppose." I smiled and went on to let Jack beat me by using the Q in QUARTZY.

Jack open the Scrabble box and began to put away the tiles and fold the game board closed. "Hey listen," he said. "I've been meaning to ask you about something. What would you say to spending Christmas with me and my family? I'm hosting Christmas here this year, but only two of my kids and their families can make it. Evan's in Hong Kong working some business deal and Sandra is going to her in-laws'. I'm not sure we can do justice to the turkey without some help. Seems a shame for good turkey to go to waste. What do you say?"

I swallowed hard. "You know, I haven't really even discussed Christmas with Celia yet. We were so busy taking care of the house and then with work—"

"It doesn't have to be a big deal. Just my friend from a neighboring cottage celebrating the season with us."

I shook my head. "It's not that. I—"

He raised a hand. "Think about it. There's no rush. You talk with your daughter and figure out what her family's plans are. Just know the offer is open." He smiled. "And I'd really like you to accept."

I smiled. "Okay. I'll think about it."

After he left, I cleared away the dishes and sat down on the sofa with the novel I'd been reading. I picked up the letter from

Alfie and read it again. I tried reading the novel after that, but I couldn't concentrate. I found myself staring into the flames of the fire still burning in the fireplace. My mind traveled back to the day that had changed everything.

It had been another day with weather not unlike today's. I was a new mom and chronically exhausted. I'd just put Celia down for her afternoon nap. I wanted to nap along with her, but there was work to do, and I hoped I might spend a little time painting if I finished in time. And if she slept long enough.

I switched the kettle on and jogged downstairs to the basement to start one more load of Alfie's work clothes before I set to work on folding the clean, dry ones. I put everything in the machine then sighed and pulled it all out again. I'd forgotten to check the pockets. I'd skip the step of soaking everything today. It didn't look too bad. I'd never seen such dirty clothes as Alfie wore home from his job as a timber feller at Roth and Sons Logging. I cringed to think how he often stopped at the bar on his way home from work in those dirty clothes. "You mean people *saw* you like this in a public place?" I'd ask him.

"A public place? You mean the bar? It's not like it's a five-star restaurant or anything, Adele. Half the boys with me are from work anyway. We all look the same."

"Well, at least you're in good company, then." I'd kiss him on his dirty cheek and send him to the shower.

"The boys" Alfie referred to were hardworking, honest men, if not a little rough around the edges—like my Alfie.

Bar nights were usually spent at a place in the next town over, on the way home to Point-du-Fleuve from the worksite. The boys would play a little pool or darts and mostly talk and burn off whatever energy they had left after the heavy labor of their workday was over. I didn't mind his having that time once a week. I was often so tired by Friday night, I relished the chance to crawl in bed early and sleep late the next morning while Alfie took care of Celia's first feeding. Since she was born, it seemed I could sleep forever if given the opportunity.

I reached into the pocket of one of the sets of work pants and pulled out close to a dollar in change and a few small bills and dropped it in a jar on the shelf over the washing machine. It was a running joke between us that I could fund an exotic vacation on the money he left in his pockets. One day while I was in the basement switching loads from the washer to the dryer, he came down with an oversized pickle jar and challenged me to do it. Now the jar was almost half full.

I tossed the pants into the washing machine and moved to the next item—one of the shirts. From the pocket I pulled a napkin. I shook my head. What on earth was he doing with a napkin shoved in the pocket? I wadded it up and prepared to throw it in the garbage when I saw something written on it. I dropped the shirt back into the basket and unfolded the napkin. A name in swirly handwriting: Linda. There was a little heart over the "i." And a phone number.

The room seemed to close in. I stared at the handwriting. What was I looking at? Why would this woman give Alfie her phone number? More importantly, why would Alfie keep it? My mind reeled.

I checked every other pocket in the remaining laundry and double-checked the ones in the clothes already in the machine. I don't know what I was looking for. Something to make sense of this. Something that said this wasn't what it looked like.

I trudged back upstairs and sat down to fold the clean laundry. I worked like a machine, my body following the familiar motions to fold each pair of pants, each shirt, each tiny cloth diaper, undershirt, and jumper while my mind spun with a million confusing thoughts.

Who was this Linda? Was Alfie having an affair? With someone at the bar? I'd thought it was just the guys getting together for some harmless fun every Friday night. Had I been naïve all this time while Alfie snuck around, right under my nose?

And now that I knew, what should I do about it? What did women do when they found themselves in this position? Should I confront him about it the minute he walked in the door? Or sit on it a few days while I watched him to see if there were signs I had been missing—behaviors I hadn't known to look for?

Or should I figure out who this Linda was? See what I was up against? This last option didn't sound right at all. If Alfie had something going on with someone else ...

I shuddered and looked up to realize the afternoon sun had faded and the house was getting cool. I should have built a fire at least an hour ago to give it a chance to heat up the house for the cold evening and night ahead.

I tiptoed down the hall again and cracked open the door to Celia's room. I didn't want to wake her, even though she'd surely wake soon on her own. But if the house was cool, I should check to see if she still had a blanket over her. I stared at her chubby little form under the soft pink blanket Mama had crocheted for her, watched the steady rise and fall of her chest. My precious baby. How little she knew of how complicated my life had become in the last hour.

A lump rose in my throat and a tear spilled down my cheek. An old fear, like an unwanted but familiar guest crept into my mind. I pictured Hannah, radiant in the violet bridesmaid's dress Mama had made. Her pleading eyes. Her soothing tone of voice. She had convinced me that there was nothing to worry about. That Alfie was the man I'd always dreamed of. She'd told me to put to rest the concerns that had threatened to choke me. Had she been wrong? Had I been wrong to listen? What if the Alfie his groomsmen had toasted that night was the real Alfie and the one I'd been living with these past four years was an act he'd managed to sustain until now? Worse yet, what if he hadn't sustained it at all—just hidden it under the façade of faithful husband and father?

I returned to the living room and knelt in front of the fireplace. I pulled some logs from the hearth and stacked them across the fire grate, larger ones on the bottom, then smaller ones in the opposite direction on top. Finally, I laid down the layer of kindling and balled up some newspapers, struck a match and it sprang to life, burning last week's obituaries and want ads. Some of the kindling tumbled down and I grabbed the poker and shoved it back into place. Alfie always appreciated my "campfire girl" skills, as he called them. He was fond of saying how well I could take care of myself—something I had prided myself on before I met him. Would I have to return to that? Would I become the sole provider for my baby and me? Would he leave me? Or would I leave first and prevent him from having the chance? If he was having an affair, I wouldn't hang around, waiting for the inevitable.

Gravel crunched in the driveway and Celia woke, almost at the same moment, so when Alfie walked in the door, I had my hands full with a diaper change.

"Hey there. How are my two favorite ladies?" Alfie called from the other room. Although it was wasn't yet twilight, Alfie was actually a little later getting home than usual. He liked to get home early since he had to be up around four in the morning—the life of a logger. But he loved the fact that it kept him outdoors and it was never dull—to say the least. His work was actually rather dangers—a fact he downplayed for my sake. He couldn't hide all the facts though. It was hard to miss when one of his crew died the year before. He'd been helping to load a truck, and one of the logs tumbled down and hit him on the head.

I couldn't help wondering what had kept Alfie this afternoon. Had he made a stop on the way home to see Linda? Or someone else?

Alfie came into Celia's room just as I was buttoning the last snap on a fresh one-piece with a cute ruffle across the front. He tickled Celia's belly and cooed at her, "So, how was Mommy's day today? Did you keep her busy? Or did she get a chance to put her feet up?"

Celia gave him a gummy smile.

"Hmmm ... that looks like mischief. My guess is Mommy didn't get a moment's rest. Did she?" He tickled her tummy again, then turned to me. "Did she?"

I handed the baby to him, avoiding his attempt to bend down and kiss my forehead. "She did not. And I'd better go check on supper. I have a roast slow-cooking."

"A roast?"

I knew what he was going to say. That I didn't have to go to such a fuss. But try as I might, even after four years of marriage, I couldn't seem to adjust to the idea that I was cooking for just the two of us—not Papa, Mama, Hannah, and me. And I liked leftovers just fine. Plus it gave me something warm to pack into Alfie's thermos for lunch each day. I worried about his not getting enough good, warm food to eat when the days grew colder—at least I had when I didn't suspect he was finding other ways to keep warm.

I plunged a knife and fork into the roast, pulled the meat apart and examined it to see if the juices ran clear—the way Mama had taught me to test for doneness—then poked the fork at a potato and a carrot. Everything seemed just about done. Steps away in the living room, Alfie had Celia on her tummy on a blanket on the floor. He lay on one side, propped up by his arm, and chatted with her as though she could understand his every word. In response she made happy little squeals and gurgling noises, flailing her arms and legs as though she were swimming the 100-meter butterfly. Every so often, she took her little fist and pummeled her daddy in the mouth with it. He opened his mouth and kissed her all over her hand. More squeals and giggles. My heart melted.

If Alfie was cheating on me, he wasn't making it easy to detect. I'd have to be direct. I had no choice but to confront him with the evidence and see where it went.

———

That evening, after Celia was tucked in bed and the supper dishes were washed and dried, I sat down on the bed just as Alfie was changing. "We need to talk."

"What's wrong?" Alfie's brow knit.

"Why do you think something's wrong?"

"You look serious. Your mom okay?"

I nodded. I had pictured this scene a little differently—me the one in control and him off-balance. But like it or not, he still had that affect on me. I reached in my pocket and pulled out the napkin. "I found this."

"A napkin?" He pulled open the dresser drawer where he kept his pajamas. "Do you feel like the house is a little cool this evening?"

"Oh yeah. I started the fire a little later this afternoon. I got … distracted." I pushed down my frustration at the change of subject. I would not be derailed. "So the napkin. The thing is, it's not just a napkin. There's a woman's number written on it."

Comprehension suddenly lit on his face. "Oh, right. Linda."

"'Oh, right, Linda?'"

He shook his head and waved a hand in the direction of the napkin. "Waitress at the bar. She's got some problem with her car. Sounds like the alternator if you ask me. She wanted my guy Brian to have a look at it."

"So she gave you her number on a napkin?" I stared at his face, trying to play detective. I wished I knew what exactly to look for.

"Yeah. You know Brian just works out of his garage at home. And I didn't remember his number. So she gave me hers, asked me to get her in touch with him." He pulled on his pajamas and threw back the covers on the bed. "You comin' to bed? Gonna help warm me up?" He grinned.

I wouldn't be dissuaded. "So she writes her name and number on a napkin so you can put her in touch with the mechanic. Then what's with the little heart?"

"Huh?"

"She writes her name with a little heart over the 'i.' See?" I held out the napkin to him.

Alfie sat up. "Adele? What gives? What's with all the questions?"

"How did this Linda know about Brian?"

Alfie shook his head. "I dunno. I guess me and the boys were talking about car repairs or something." He scratched his head. "Yeah, that was it. Patty said somethin' about his car needing some work, and we got talking about who you could trust, you know. And I mentioned Brian. I guess she was sitting down with us at that point."

I raised my eyebrows at that. "She sits down with you guys? I thought your nights at the bar were guys-only."

He shrugged dismissively. "It's not like we make an announcement. But it's just us guys that meet at the bar together. Occasionally a woman comes in one of the guys knows. Or Linda. But it's no big deal."

"No big deal?"

"Yeah. No big deal." Alfie reached for my hand. "Adele, what's going on here? You okay?"

I sighed, exasperated. "Alfie, women don't write their names on napkins with little hearts for mechanic referrals."

"What?" He blinked at me.

I thrust the napkin at him. "Just look. See the way she signs her name?" I stared at all the curly-cues and that stupid little heart as I held it out to him.

He looked at the napkin. "Okay …"

"Tell me this. She's a flirt, right?"

He stopped and seemed to consider the idea a moment. "Yeah, I guess you could say she's a bit of a flirt."

I threw up my hands. "You see?"

Alfie looked at the clock. "No, honey, I don't see. And I need to get to sleep. Four a.m. comes awful early. Come to bed. Can we talk about this another time?"

I undressed slowly, still pondering our frustrating conversation, and climbed into the cold bed. Alfie was already sound asleep. I lay awake for at least another hour puzzling over the events of the day and listening to him snore. As far as I could tell, Alfie didn't seem to be hiding anything. But I couldn't be sure.

He had given what *he* seemed to think was a rational explanation for the presence of the napkin in his pocket. But no matter how I turned the matter over in my head, I couldn't put it to rest. Whether Alfie's intentions were innocent or not, Linda's certainly weren't. Of that much I was certain.

That left only two possibilities: either Alfie was downplaying Linda's flirtations because he was hiding whatever was going on between them. Or he truly didn't see that she had designs on him. Either he was a liar and cheating on me, or he was unwitting prey. Neither thought gave me much comfort as I drifted into exhausted sleep.

I shivered and glanced at the clock as my mind returned to the present. Just how long had I been sitting here, carried away by my thoughts? The fire had burned down to just the embers. I turned off the light and headed down the hall to bed, leaving the novel and the letter on the coffee table for another day.

The memory of that long-ago day floated back to me as I drew down the covers. How many times had I accused Alfie of indiscretions? He denied it, every time. Looking back, I realized that in the early days, he truly was innocent—at least of any intent toward infidelity if not of the intent to place himself in questionable situations.

After a while, whether because he kept returning to those situations or because he grew weary of being accused of something he didn't actually do without anything to show for it, there came a day he confessed there had indeed been someone else.

There was little sense of victory in being proven right.

He swore he'd change and that it had been the first time, but my nagging and paranoia only increased. In the end it was hard to decide who had been more responsible for the dissolution of our marriage, though Alfie was the one who finally decided to leave.

One of the saddest things about life is our ability to see these things clearly only in hindsight.

The day Alfie left, early in the morning without even causing me to stir in the bed, was the day I had decided for good on the truth of that German proverb. True love really was illusive as a ghost.

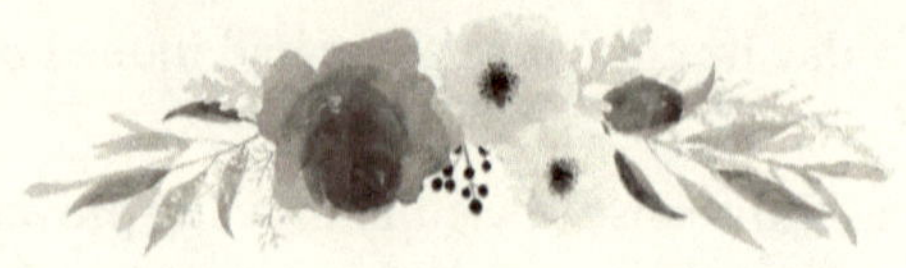

The house was warm with the spicy aromas of hot apple cider and pine. The timer went off, and I bumped into Celia on the way to the oven to retrieve the pies—mincemeat and pumpkin.

Celia laughed. "I know it's frustrating the house hasn't sold yet, but it's nice we get to spend one more Christmas in it, don't you think?"

"I can't say I'm sorry." I pulled the pies out of the oven and set them on the counter.

Caleb ran in from the other room. "When's dinner, Gramma? Daddy told me to ask. Is it ready yet?" He reached up to sneak a bit of turkey from the serving platter, then looked at me, his eyes begging permission.

"Daddy told you to ask, did he?" I peered into the living room where Jeff sat nodding on the sofa in front of a football game. "Take one piece. Just don't tell your mother," I whispered.

"I heard that," Celia called over her shoulder from her post at the stove, stirring the gravy.

I was glad to enjoy this last Christmas in the home Celia

and I had shared for so many years. I had considered Jack's request. I really had. But when the real estate agent called to say he was sorry the house hadn't sold and advised delisting it and waiting to try again in the spring, it did feel like Christmas in the old house was meant to be. With its new coat of paint and stripped of the old wallpaper, the house really did look fresh and lovely. It would be even harder to say goodbye to it.

Jack said he understood. And that Evan would be home for Christmas after all, so there would be less turkey to go around anyway. But it was hard to miss the disappointment in his voice or the way he barely met my eyes.

We'd promised to get together for another games night in the new year though. I looked forward to it.

Celia looked over her shoulder again and grabbed Caleb's hand just as he reached for another bite of turkey. "Wait until it's served, young man. In about ten minutes, right Mom?"

I nodded. "Should be. Let's see, you're working on the gravy, cranberry sauce is in the fridge, stuffing's in the warmer ... what am I forgetting?"

"The beans."

"The beans. I haven't even topped and tailed them yet. Would you help?"

Celia stood beside me at the sink as we each snapped the beans into bite-sized pieces, took the ends off, and dropped the green beans into a colander. "So, back in the summer, you were telling me about a certain neighbor of yours. What's been happening there?"

"You mean Jack?"

Celia gave me an exasperated look. "Of course I mean Jack. Or do you have all the men in your neighborhood lined up at your door?"

Well, not quite, but more suitors than I could manage at the moment, anyway. In addition to deflecting Jack's advances, I had left Alfie's letter unanswered, figuring there was no point in writing so close to the holidays. There was no rush in answering him—if I ever did.

"We've been getting together here and there."

"And?" Celia snapped the last of the beans in two pieces and ran them under cold water. "Here. Do you want to steam them?"

I shrugged. "There's not much to tell."

Celia faced me, a hand on her hip. "Mom, don't you go and mess this up."

I smiled, doing my best to be casual. "Don't be silly. There's nothing to mess up. We're old friends."

"Is that what he would say?"

"That's what he was planning on telling his kids—"

A smile spread across her face, and she leaned in closer, her voice low. "He told his kids about you?"

I waved my hand at her. "No, no. I mean, I don't know. It's just—"

"What?"

"It's nothing. He invited me to spend Christmas with his family, but of course I couldn't accept. I wouldn't miss Christmas with you and Jeff and Caleb."

Just then Caleb tore into the kitchen and hovered near the turkey. "Did you call me, Gramma? Is it ten minutes yet? I washed my hands, see?" He held them out to his mother for inspection.

Celia looked them over. "Good job. Wait... what's this?" Celia held one of his pinkies between her fingers.

Caleb squinted. "That's brown marker. I drew a picture of Santa and his sleigh. It's reindeer color."

"Better go wash again."

"Aw, Mom."

"And tell Daddy to wash up too," Celia called after him as he skidded down the hallway toward the bathroom. She turned back to me. "Did you see that? If I'd called him to clean his room, he would never have heard me, but speak his name barely above a whisper when food is involved and he's here in a flash."

I laughed. "He likes his Granmma's cooking. Nothing wrong with that."

"Let's get this bird on the table." Celia lifted the turkey platter and headed toward the dining room. "But don't think we're finished with that conversation, Mom. You still haven't explained why the handsome, rich neighbor isn't good enough for you."

Knowing my daughter, she'd make good on her word. We weren't finished with that conversation. But I wouldn't be any readier for it later than I was now. I didn't know what held me back from Jack. I didn't know why true love had eluded me all these years. Nor why things hadn't worked out with Alfie for that matter. If I did, I wouldn't have spent the last thirty years alone.

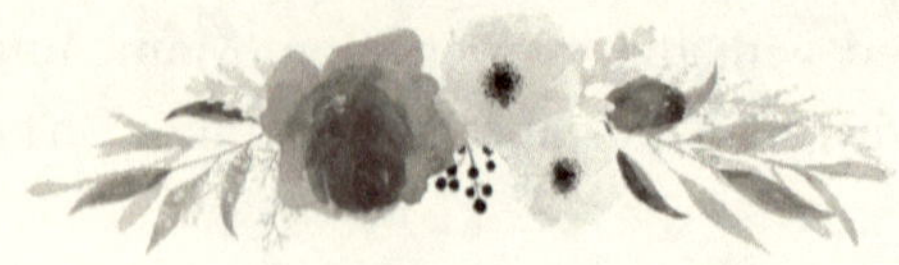

I lifted the blades from the *Weihnachtspyramide*—the Christmas pyramid my mother brought from Germany those many years ago—and placed each piece reverently in its worn box, followed by the main tower. Each piece fit perfectly into a molded section of the box that guaranteed its safety until it was needed to mark another nativity season.

I hadn't put up many other decorations in the cottage, knowing I'd spend the season with Celia and her family. After Christmas I'd taken down the tree in Point-du-Fleuve because it was real, but the ornaments hadn't been properly stored.

I'd left quickly. I wanted to return to the shop to help Jo-Ann tidy up after Christmas. And I missed the routine of my new life at the cottage. Hannah had promised to join me to finish packing up the attic before the house was relisted in the spring, and I'd figured we could deal with the Christmas things then.

I closed the lid on the box and carried it to its place at the back of a large closet Alfie had built for storage of all our seasonal things, although at the time we'd been thinking more of the summer seasonal items—oars for a canoe, life jackets, and pails and shovels for the sand. With a sigh, I gazed at those items now. It wouldn't be long before I had to take them to Goodwill. Caleb's sandcastle-building days wouldn't last much longer.

I couldn't help thinking of Alfie and how he'd never gotten to know his grandson at all. My ex-husband had been popping into my mind more and more lately. I didn't know what to make of all his talk of changing. He was certainly the last person I'd ever have thought would turn to religion. Although the way he talked about it didn't seem religious somehow. More like God was a father. Well, of course I knew that was true. After all, wasn't that the way the Lord's Prayer started?

How strange those words had sounded when I'd shown up in Mrs. Carter's grade six classroom that first year we'd emigrated from Germany. Everyone had sung "O Canada" then prayed the Lord's Prayer. At first I had no idea what was going on, but bit by bit I realized some of the words were familiar since I'd learned to pray the prayer in German. I was so shy and scared in that classroom. So much was strange and new. Mrs. Carter would coax me to answer questions, but I was too afraid to speak. I didn't want anyone to laugh at me. The morning ritual of the prayer was the safest, most predictable part of my day. It wasn't long before I had memorized the prayer in English and could recite it fluently, even without much of an accent. One day Mrs. Carter stood near me as I spoke the familiar words. I hadn't seen her there. The look on her face when she heard me speaking almost made me laugh right at the part where we ask for our daily bread. The trouble was, Mrs. Carter assumed I could speak fluently all the time and began calling on me more and more in class.

And the other kids *did* laugh.

In the end, I'd stopped saying the prayer. I suppose I hadn't really prayed that much ever since. But Alfie's relationship with God seemed different than the "Our Father" God.

Could Alfie's God help me sort out all the tangled threads of my life? Could he show me what to do about Jack or my ex-husband? Could he help me finally find true love? Could he walk me through what to do about a house that wasn't selling or the perils of owning a business? I knew Papa would gladly help with all those things if he were still alive. Was that the kind of "Our Father" Alfie had found?

Alfie's last letter still sat on the coffee table. I'd been so frozen with indecision about what to do with it I hadn't even moved it to a better place. Maybe I should write back after all. Alfie could tell me more about his newfound religion. Or relationship. Or whatever it was he had experienced. But replying would have consequences. He'd said he wanted to keep writing me. One letter had already become two. If I wrote him back again, I would be inviting a third and a fourth and who knows how many after that. Was that really what I wanted?

And I still didn't fully understand what was behind the last two sentences of his most recent letter: *"I've missed you, Adele. Aside from the Good Lord, you were the best thing that ever happened to me."* What kind of door would I be opening if I replied?

The whole time I'd been considering all of this, I'd stood with the closet door half open, staring at but not seeing the collection of buckets and shovels. "Next thing you know, Adele, you'll be talking to yourself." I closed the door and strode to the coffee table, picked up the letter, and sat down with it at the desk. I pulled out a piece of the flowered stationery, pen poised over the paper.

I took a deep breath. "Our Father, who art in heaven ... is this a good idea? Should I write Alfie back? I don't know if you answer when people talk to you. Or if you concern yourself with little things like this—my needing to know if writing my ex-husband is a good idea or not. But I sure would appreciate some kind of sign. Or something." I listened, but the only answer was the gentle ticking of the kitchen clock.

Out on the lake, dark, muddy waves matched the foreboding winter sky, while at the shore, the wind off the lake had whipped the snow into stiff, peaked drifts. A frosting of white covered all the trees nearest the cottage. Abruptly, a sprinkling caught my attention. I expected to see a squirrel bouncing between trees, knocking snow from the branches. Instead, on the tip of a cedar branch a yellow bird sat grooming itself. It stopped, cocked its head to the side, as though regarding me, and sang out a clear note. The characteristic call of—could that really be—a cardinal?

I snatched my camera from its hook by the back door and snapped shot after shot, grateful I'd left the zoom lens on. Sure enough, it was a rare yellow northern cardinal—the existence of which I'd only recently learned about—although I'd never heard of one being spotted this far north. The bird flitted to another, higher branch but stayed where I could easily capture beautiful, clear shots. I snapped several more while it chirped insistently. Finally it flew up and over the cottage beyond my view. I lowered the camera, almost reverently, and sat in the chair by the desk.

I looked back at the desktop, where Alfie's letter lay next to the pen and flowered paper. Right before the spectacular appearance of the cardinal, I'd been wondering—no, praying about—whether I should write to him. I looked back at the branch where the bird had perched, then at the screen of my camera where the image of the last shot I'd taken still lingered.

What had just happened? Was this an answer to my prayer?

"Our Father, was that You?" I picked up the pen again and wrote.

Dear Alfie,

To be honest, I didn't expect you to write again. I'm so glad you did. Please feel free to continue to write to me. And please tell me more about your conversations with Pastor Manuel.

Adele

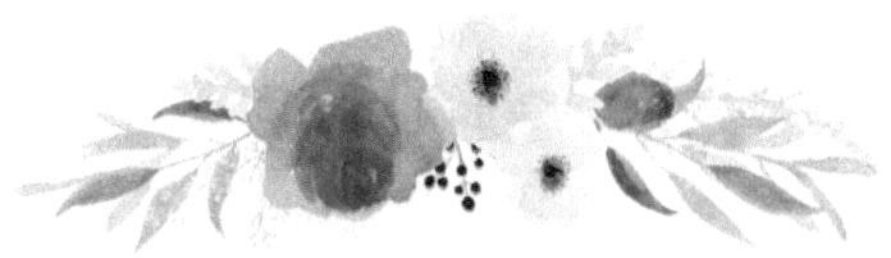

"Hand me that bunch of long-stems?" Jo-Ann reached across the table. She scowled over the glasses she wore low on the bridge of her nose. She said this was the busiest Valentine's Day she could remember in a long time. She credited it to my seasonal window display and the simple renovations I'd done to the shop. The name over the door had changed, and the change had brought in a lot of curious new customers. Some had even purchased the few watercolor and acrylic paintings I'd hung around the shop. The scenes that hung right now were all romantic snow scenes of downtown Port Sandford and a few of the lake. Two or three of my winter sunsets had sold recently, and I planned to start classes in the studio in the spring. But first we had to survive the craziness of February fourteenth.

Tina came in from the front of the shop. "Four more new delivery orders," she announced, holding up the order slips.

"Are you kidding?" Jo-Ann pushed up her glasses and peered at the orders. "And they're all big bouquets." She glanced at her watch. "I thought we set cut-off at noon."

Tina shrugged. "I figured we still had the stock and Gus hasn't gone out for his last delivery yet."

Jo-Ann handed the slips to me. "Check and make sure we have the stock to make all of these. We may have to get creative with red roses."

"Got it. I have an inventory list here somewhere. I'll check it."

"Check the fridges too. We may have forgotten to check some off in the craziness." She grinned. "Isn't this great?"

Jack would be pleased. He'd given his approval on all the changes at the shop and congratulated me regularly on what a good business move it had been to buy it. Jack and I still met for games night every Sunday evening through the winter, sometimes at his place, sometimes at mine. And ever since the anniversary of Emma's death, we'd been getting to know each other on a deeper level. He'd opened up more to me. As I had to him—although I had yet to mention my recent correspondence with Alfie, which had evolved into long conversations over the telephone. The first one had been awkward and halting—somewhat reminiscent of our occasional conversations when he still lived on the army base and I was still in my parents' home. But it had been wonderful to hear the warmth and familiar rhythm of his voice.

Those conversations had also taken an interesting turn. Alfie had honored my request to talk more about his conversations with his pastor, and I had begun reading a Bible. I'd had to buy one at the bookshop down the street from Every Bloomin' Thing because the only one I could find around the cottage was Mama's old German Bible and my German had gotten far too rusty for that. Alfie and I talked about the Bible, about our shared memories, and kept each other abreast about what was going on in our lives—although I didn't mention anything about Jack to Alfie either.

Sometimes the irony of the situation seemed almost

humorous to me. I'd remained single without a suitor for thirty years, and suddenly two men were looking for my attention. For the most part, I'd kept them both successfully at bay since I still hadn't sorted out my feelings for either of them. But it was feeling more and more like a difficult juggling act.

I checked the inventory list against what was in the fridge. Jo-Ann was right. There was a discrepancy, but it was in our favor. We'd have enough to finish these arrangements and some extra in case there were last-minute walk-ins for single stems. I glanced at the clock. It was later than I thought. We should be just fine. As I slid the refrigerator door closed, I noticed two of our Valentine's special arrangements on the shelf. One was the regular special and the other one a deluxe with extra roses and the addition of stephanotis. Why hadn't they gone out for delivery yet? I leaned in a little closer, checking for their delivery tags. There were none. I slid the door closed and returned to the back room.

"Those two Valentine's specials in the fridge. Who are they for? There are no delivery tags."

"Oh those. I'm delivering them myself at closing. Don't worry."

"Neither one of them has a To/From card either.'

Jo-Ann looked up and peered at me over her glasses. She needed bifocals but refused to buy them. "I may be retiring, but I refuse to admit that I'm old," she would say. "You're right. Thanks for the reminder."

I returned to my station and continued working on the arrangement I'd been working on. Another Valentine's special. Jo-Ann and I had designed the arrangement together, and it had been wildly popular. Roses, buttercups, stephanotis, and gardenia. With a heart-shaped card surrounded by real lace.

A gust of frosty air blew in the back door as Gus, the delivery man, walked in. More than a few snowflakes followed him through the door. It had been snowing steadily all day.

"Hey, Gus," Jo-Ann waved. "Last of the deliveries are right over there on the table. Adele and I just need to get these last two wrapped up, and this should be your last run. Why don't you help yourself to some of that hot chocolate Tina made and get warmed up while you wait?"

"Sounds good to me," Gus said, already pulling a mug down from the shelf.

"How's the weather out there?"

"Still coming down."

"I just love a snowy Valentine's Day, don't you?" Jo-Ann clipped a stem as though for emphasis.

I nodded. "So romantic."

Gus snorted. "You can say that all you want from in here. Those roads are gettin' pretty slick."

"Well, take your time, Gus. These are all the last-minute Valentine's people. They should have planned better if they wanted you to risk your life for their flowers."

Gus raised his mug and grinned. "You got that right, Boss."

Jo-Ann and I finished our arrangements at almost the same time and put them on the table with the rest of them. Gus put his coat back on, and we helped him load the van. Jo-Ann closed the back door and rubbed her hands together. "Chilly out there. Tina, you can go on home whenever you want, sweetie.'

"Yes, thanks for all your help today," I said. "We couldn't have done it without you."

Jo-Ann looked at me and motioned toward the table with all the snippings and ribbon, wrapping paper, and cards lying strewn about. Evidence of a profitable day. "All this can wait until tomorrow. Why don't we sit down and have a hot chocolate? I have something for you."

I raised an eyebrow. "For me? Candy hearts? You want to be my valentine?"

She laughed. She and I had agreed to have dinner together

at the diner in town. We knew we would both be too tired to go home and fix a meal. And we'd decided spending it with each other would be far better than eating alone on Valentine's Day. Knowing that all the nicer restaurants in town would be filled with young lovers, we'd settled on the diner.

She disappeared to the front of the shop for a moment while I poured our mugs of hot chocolate and returned carrying both the Valentine specials I'd seen in the fridge earlier. She reached carefully inside the cellophane and put the To/From cards inside each arrangement. "These, my dear friend, are for you. I have a feeling there's a whole lot you haven't been telling me. The Deluxe is from Jack, and this one is from someone named Alfie."

18

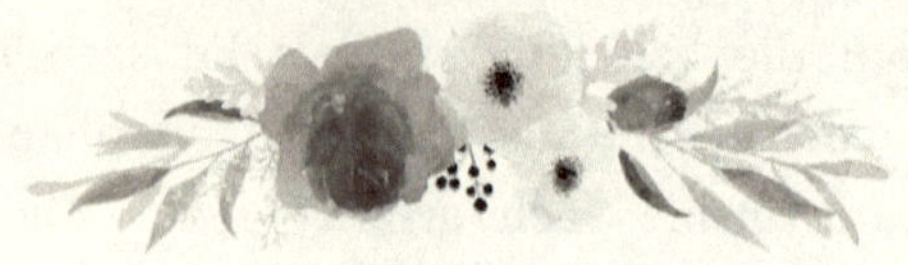

The next day was Sunday with few customers. Jo-Ann and I spent the better part of the morning cleaning up the Valentine's Day fallout. We decided to close early when the snow started up again and we'd had only two or three customers all afternoon.

I told her over dinner the night before of course. About Jack and what had—or hadn't—been going on with him since he'd expressed his interest back in the summer. About the day I'd caught him grieving for Emma. About games night and how I'd become very fond of him. I also told her about Alfie, his letters, and phone calls. And the restoration that seemed to be happening in that relationship.

Jo-Ann listened, nodding at the right parts, shaking her head at others, every once in a while, putting a hand on my arm in empathy or waiting while I found the right words to express the confusion I'd felt over the last number of months. It was such a relief to be able to talk to someone about all of it. There had been no one else to confide in.

Celia still regularly grilled me about Jack, but she knew nothing at all about Alfie coming back into my life. And I knew that was the way it had to stay. Which made my feelings for him even more confusing.

I knew I could trust Hannah with all of it, but I was afraid to. She'd encouraged me to stick it out with Alfie, and I always felt I'd disappointed her when we split up. I just didn't have the heart to talk to her about it now.

That evening, I went home and made Fettuccine Alfredo for dinner—Jack's favorite—and pulled the games from their shelf in the living room beside the fireplace. I picked up the bouquet of flowers from Alfie, carried it to my bedroom, put it on the dresser, and closed the door.

Jack arrived, right on time, and there was a moment or two of awkwardness as I stumbled out a thank-you for the flowers. "They're beautiful," I said. "It was a nice surprise."

"It's hard keeping this kind of thing a secret from a woman who works at a flower shop." He chuckled. "Jo-Ann was a real sport."

"It was very sweet of you."

He stepped closer.

I dodged and headed to the kitchen. "The salad's not on the table yet, and I need to pour the sauce over the pasta." I suddenly wished I hadn't made his favorite dish. It had been years since Mama had died, yet in that moment I heard her voice clearly, "*Liebe geht durch den Magen*"—the German version of, "the way to a man's heart is through his stomach." What had I been thinking?

Jack joined me in the kitchen. "I can help."

"It's okay. Just have a seat. I'll have it ready in a moment." But I dropped the strainer trying to pour the water from the pasta and he came and held it for me.

"Thank you." A strangled laugh escaped from my throat. "I seem to be all thumbs."

We sat at the table, and he poured glasses of wine for each of us. "It smells wonderful. Fettuccine Alfredo. You remembered."

I smiled, wishing I could be coy or play dumb. I'd never been good at that. "Of course I remembered." The room seemed too quiet, yet I hadn't wanted to turn on music, not anxious to create any sort of mood. Nevertheless, the tension in the room was tangible. There was a mood already at work. How could I derail it?

Jack studied my face a moment or two then took a bite of the pasta. "Delicious," he pronounced. "How was work today?"

I breathed a sigh of relief. "Quiet. The weather, I guess. And everyone's already spent their money on Valentine's Day."

He nodded. And was either oblivious to the fact that I'd just invited talk of romance again or pretended to be.

Things stayed light through the rest of the meal. Jack asked about Celia and Caleb and told me about his daughter's children, who had plans to visit during spring break. "I hope they're not disappointed," he said. "They usually head down to Florida every year, but this year Steve's got something at work and can't get away. My place is definitely second-best."

"Oh, don't be silly. They always enjoy visiting in the summer, don't they?"

"Sure, but in the summer, they can swim or take the canoe out or waterski." He took a sip of the wine. "It'll be all grandpa, all the time. Not much else to do."

"You're welcome to my board game collection."

"They're not really board game people."

I frowned. "How can that be? You and Emma must have failed to pass down that gene somehow."

He smiled. "The truth is, the real game player in our family was Emma. I only played because she enjoyed it."

I lowered my fork. "Are you serious?"

He shrugged. "Yes."

"But all these months you've been joining me for games. You didn't enjoy it? Why didn't you say something?"

"I did enjoy it. Just like I enjoyed playing with Emma. It's the company, not the activity."

I blushed, pretty certain it wasn't the wine. I opened my mouth and closed it again. "I don't know what to say. I guess this means you don't want to keep it up, then?"

"If you enjoy it, I enjoy it. I was happy for the excuse to be with you. I've enjoyed every week this winter coming over here or having you at my place." He took my hand across the table. "I know you've wanted your space, Adele. And I've done my best to respect that. I don't want to rush you into something you're not ready for. But it's been a few months now. We've gotten to know each other better, and I was thinking ... well, I was hoping we could move things to another level."

My mouth went dry. I wanted to stop the rush of his words, but I had no idea what I could say to make that happen.

"I was hoping you felt the same as I do, Adele. Please tell me you do."

I opened my mouth to say something—I wasn't sure yet exactly what—and the phone rang.

I winced. "I'm sorry. Excuse me." I ran to the phone. The voice on the other end of the line was Alfie's. "Adele? Can you hear me?"

Jack stood and began to clear away our dinner dishes. I held up a finger to let him know I would only be a minute.

"Can I call you back?"

"Oh. Uh, let me see. I've got a new cell phone. Dropped the old one. I don't know the new number. Hang on a minute."

I tuned in closer to the phone line. I could hear noise in the background, as though he were standing outside somewhere. "Why don't you just call tomorrow? Hello? Oh. You're not there." I cast a rueful glance toward Jack, who was now running a sink of water for the dishes.

"Did you say something? I was gettin' the number for you.

It's dead now. Just charging. I wrote the number down on a piece of paper, though. Got a pen?"

"Sure, just a moment. Or you can call me tomorrow?"

"Sorry, what's that?

"Never mind. I have a pen. Go ahead." I scribbled the number on a piece of paper.

"Okay. I've got some news too. I'll be changing routes to the Midwest. Which probably means I'll be moving. But call me when you can."

"I will. Talk soon. Goodbye." I hung up the phone.

Jack looked up from the wine glass he was washing. "Celia?"

"No. An old friend. We'll talk another time."

The room grew quiet but for the crackle of the fire. "Jack—"

He spoke at the same moment. He put down the washcloth, dried his hands and came close. "Adele, I'm sorry I rushed you. It's plain to see you need more time." He chuckled softly. "But we're not getting any younger, you and I. And I'll confess that feeling the way I do about you, getting together once a week to play games—as much as I've enjoyed your company all this time—well ... it's not enough anymore."

He bent and kissed me gently on my forehead. "I'll give you more time to think about your answer, but in the meantime, let's take a break on games night, okay?"

I nodded and blinked away the tears that welled in my eyes. "I'm sorry, Jack. Maybe when things settle down with the business and the house, I'll be able to think more clearly about all this ..."

"Still no movement on the house?"

I shook my head. "Realtor says to wait until spring."

We finished tidying up together, talking about safe topics, like our children and grandchildren, the weather, my painting, and the mounting number of summer weddings the shop had been booking for flower arrangements and bouquets. A half hour later Jack left, lingering briefly at the door while he seemed to be deciding whether or not to kiss me.

"Goodbye, Adele. I love you," he whispered, his voice barely audible over the waves. He turned and walked off into the frosty night.

19

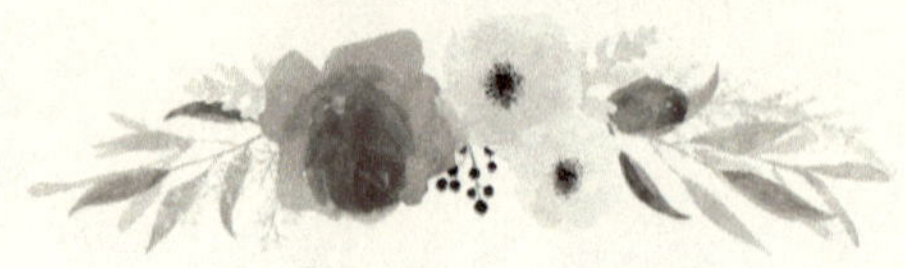

Spring came. It was strange and a little lonely not seeing Jack every week. And awkward when we met coming and going on the lane or along the beach while he took Pepper for his daily walks. I found myself looking forward more and more to Alfie's phone calls. But I hadn't been able to sort out whether I longed to hear his voice more because of Jack's absence or because the familiar bond between us was growing stronger once again. And I certainly hadn't been able to work through the nature of my feelings for either of them.

Jo-Ann and I met with more and more young couples planning their weddings. From time to time I spotted that look in the eyes of the bride-to-be that I once believed to be the look of true love. I couldn't help but think of the old photo of Mama and Papa—and the newer one of Alfie and me.

The trees outside burst with fresh green leaves. Crocuses popped up all around the cottage. I spent my evenings painting a fresh supply of paintings to sell at the shop and finally started booking my first watercolor classes.

And then the realtor called and asked me to return to Point-du-Fleuve to make the final steps to ready the house for sale.

118

There were still a few belongings that needed to find a place in the cottage, and I needed to give the whole house a final cleaning. Hannah met me in the driveway. "I'll wait until we get inside for my hug," she said, holding up hands full of buckets, rags, and a mop. "And I have something for you."

"I can see that."

"I mean something else. Something I found in Mama's old trunk."

"More treasures?"

Crocuses were just starting to pop up in the front garden at the old house too. I sighed. "I'll miss these gardens."

"Now don't go getting sentimental. We've got work to do. And you're trading this in for a lake and that cute little flower shop. And less snow in the winter. You're getting the better end of the deal." She grinned. "Now put me to work."

We worked for a couple of hours packing the remaining belongings into my car and then started cleaning everything. Just before noon, the real estate agent showed up and for the second time, drove the for-sale sign into the ground in the front yard.

"It's really happening." I swallowed the lump in my throat. Celia and I had shared so many memories here—good and bad. Somehow the moment deserved more ceremony.

Hannah loaded the buckets and mop into the back of her car. "Why don't you follow me back to my place? I have some soup in the crockpot and some fresh biscuits we can heat up for lunch."

"Sounds good."

I followed Hannah's car through the familiar streets of Point-du-Fleuve. As much as she tried to dismiss my sentimentality, it was strange to be leaving the town we'd grown up in. The town I'd raised my daughter in. The town I'd met Alfie in. My thoughts wandered to him and my heart warmed. I'd begun to think it would be nice to see him again.

I turned in at Hannah's driveway and we went inside where the smells of her pumpkin soup filled the house. Her recipe rivaled any I'd tasted anywhere else. We'd worked up quite an appetite with our labors and made short work of a couple of bowls each and the warmed biscuits. She pushed her bowl away, stood and filled a kettle of water, and turned on the stove. She dug in her purse, and pulled out a bunch of envelopes, bound with a faded ribbon.

"What's this?" I pushed my bowl away as well.

"I told you I had something for you." She bit her lip as she held out the little package.

I reached out to take them, and she pulled them back.

"I'm not sure if you're ready for this."

"What do you mean? What are they?"

She pulled on the ribbon and released the stack of envelopes. "These are letters that Mama and Papa wrote to each other. I'm not sure why Mama saved them."

I reached for them again. "Obviously they meant something to her." I smiled. "They were so in love."

Hannah pulled them back again. "That's just the thing. They were in love. Of course they were. But things weren't as easy as we—as you—imagined."

"What is that supposed to mean?"

Hannah shrugged. "I know you've always imagined they had this amazing, perfect love."

I sat up straight. What was she implying? "I didn't imagine anything. I know it. They were in love. You only needed to look at them. To listen to Mama talk."

Hannah looked down at the stack of letters. She nodded. "You're right. She was devoted to him. But after you and Alfie were married, I saw things—"

"Things?"

"Little things. Little comments Mama would make. Some subtle things in the dynamic between them. Nothing I could have easily put a finger on. Just a kind of vibe I picked up on from time to time."

"A vibe? Really Hannah, you sound like Celia's friend Sarah with all her New Age nonsense." I sat back and folded my arms.

Hannah touched my arm. "Don't be like that. I'm not doing the best job of explaining, I know. But, well, here ..." She unfolded one of the envelopes and withdrew a yellowed letter. "Listen to this. My German's not so good, but I can make it out. She read out the words in her heavily accented German.

Dear Dieter,

It's been two months since you left. Adele asks for you every day. Even little Hannah misses you and calls out "Papa" when she thinks she hears something at the door. Please come home. I was angry when you told me about that other woman, but if you come home now, I promise that all is forgiven. I want us to be a family again—

I snatched the letter from her. "You're right. Your German isn't very good. Let me have a look." I read the words in my mother's familiar cursive, wishing them—willing them—to be different from what Hannah had read aloud. But it turned out Hannah's German wasn't as bad as she thought.

My mind whirled, and the scene of my parents dancing in the kitchen came rushing back to me. This time the scene froze at that single tear on Mama's cheek. Suddenly a million little moments from my childhood swirled before me, and I saw just what Hannah meant: the dynamic I'd somehow missed.

Everything I thought to be true was crashing down around me. If my parents' love hadn't been true love, what was? Did such a thing even exist?

Hannah touched my arm again. She spoke, and her voice was soft and gentle. "Adele, it doesn't mean they didn't love each other. It just means that they were human. So their love wasn't some fairy-tale romance. It was real. But they stuck at it. They eventually made it work, didn't they? They stayed together 'til death did them part. You saw the way Mama looked at Papa when he was dying. You heard the things he said to her. Every good marriage takes hard work. Like my marriage with Michael." She leaned in closer until my gaze met hers. "Maybe even like yours and Alfie's?"

"It sounds like Papa cheated on Mama." I could barely choke out the words.

Hannah shook her head. "We'll never know for sure. But you're right. It could be."

I stared into her eyes. "Has Michael cheated on you?"

"No."

"Could you forgive that?"

She took a deep breath and released it slowly. "Honestly, I hope I never have to find out. But Mama did ... And you have, haven't you?"

I smiled sadly.

"There's another one you should see." Hannah pulled another envelope from the stack and unfolded the letter inside. "This one's from Papa to Mama.

Dearest Else,

I want to tell you I'm sorry, but it doesn't sound like enough. I've been doing a lot of thinking lately and praying. And I read this: Love is patient and kind; love does not envy or boast; it is not arrogant or rude. It does not insist on its own way; it is not irritable or resentful; it does not rejoice at wrongdoing but rejoices with the truth. Love bears all things, believes all things, hopes all things, endures all things. Love never ends—'

"The minister read that at our wedding."

"I know. I remember."

"That doesn't sound easy—that kind of love."

Hannah nodded. "Right. Marriage—love—takes hard work. No one said it would be easy."

"A good friend told me that recently." I thought about that conversation with Jack and what he'd said about Emma. He'd stuck with it. He'd changed. Had I had it wrong all these years? Had I given up on my marriage, holding on to a fairy tale idea of romance? "You're right, you know. I forgave him long ago."

The kettle on the stove began to whistle. Hannah stood and made a pot of tea and brought it to the table, along with two large mugs.

"You know, he and I have been talking again."

Hannah's face lit up. "Alfie? Really?"

I nodded. "He wrote me last summer and asked me to forgive him. He's changed a lot. He wanted to let me know and to tell me he was sorry."

Hannah reached around and hugged me, nearly knocking over one of the mugs. "Oh, Adele. I'm so happy to hear it."

"My neighbor Jack has also been romancing me."

She looked down at her lap. "Yes, I know. Celia mentioned it."

I sat back. "So, explain yourself. You're not happy to hear about the neighbor Celia has decided is the right thing for me, but you're thrilled to hear that my ex-husband is back in touch?"

She blushed. "I don't know how to explain it. Ever since you and Alfie met, I've felt he was a good man—the right one for you." She poured us each a cup of tea. "I'll never forget our conversation in the bathroom on your wedding day."

"Nor will I."

"I was convinced Alfie was your one true love."

"Now who's sounding hopelessly romantic?" I took a long sip of the tea.

She laughed. "I know. But it's true. I've always felt that way. When you were struggling, I still believed it. And when you divorced, I felt like I should stay quiet. But I never stopped believing that Alfie loved you and that if you worked at it—gave it the hard work that a marriage needs—that the two of you could be happy together." She took a sip of the tea. "I could see it in his eyes."

"In *his* eyes?"

"Oh yeah. You couldn't miss it. He had a way of looking at you that let everyone know you were the only woman in the room—the only woman in the world. Surely you know what I'm talking about."

Suddenly I couldn't wait to get home and dig out that old photograph. What had I missed? How could I not have seen what Hannah saw? And how could I have been so wrong? What if all these years everything Alfie and I had needed to make love work was right there between us? Yes, he'd made some mistakes, but it was my anger and distrust that kept him away —maybe even what pushed him away in the first place. I knew that. I'd been beginning to recognize it as we had renewed our friendship over the last few months.

I wiped away a tear. "Thank you for sharing these with me. Can I take them?"

"Of course." Hannah tied the ribbon around the stack of envelopes again and handed them to me. "I think she wanted you to have them. She saved them in that trunk for some reason, didn't she?"

My heart warmed. And yet it was a curious thought—that these clues to the truth about my parents' marriage had sat in my attic all these years waiting for me to unravel them. How much grief could I have saved myself if I'd looked at them sooner? What if I'd understood what my mother understood all those years ago about making marriage work—about the real nature of true love? How different might the last thirty years have been?

As though she were reading my mind, Hannah spoke again.

"Isn't it interesting how the truth finds us at the moment we're ready for it?"

I poured more tea into both our mugs. "You remember in the bathroom on my wedding day, you promised one day *I'd* get to be the big sister, full of sage advice?"

Hannah laughed. "I remember."

"So, when exactly will that day come?"

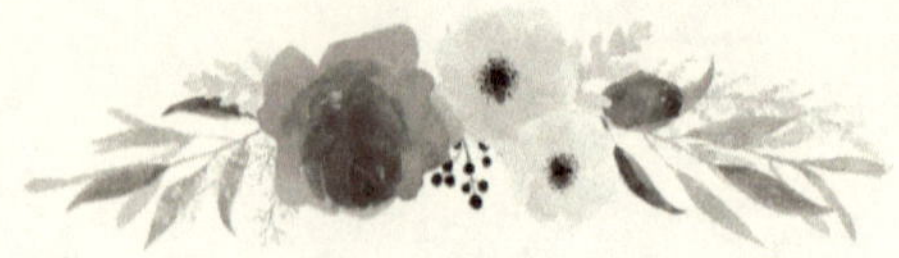

Jo-Ann and I had been busy preparing a quote for the Kowalski-Gupta wedding when I received a call that there was a firm offer on the house. After work, that evening I drove into the driveway and spotted Jack walking Pepper along the beach. I waved and he waved back. We met on the patio slab outside my back door.

"I thought you'd like to hear the news. My house sold today. I'll have to go up and sign the paperwork, but there's a firm offer and the buyer's financing checks out."

Jack beamed. "That's wonderful news." His eyes were warm, and I realized how much I missed seeing him smile. But I knew now, as I stared into his eyes. I knew what had held me back from embracing his offer of something more.

Hannah was right. It had always been Alfie. He'd never left my heart all these years. And she was right that I'd given up on our marriage too soon. Alfie and I had unfinished business. That unfinished business had held me back from relationships for thirty years. I owed it to him and to myself to see where things might go if given a second chance.

"Would you like to come in for some coffee or tea?"

Jack looked back over his shoulder toward his house. "I really shouldn't."

I nodded. He turned to go, and I caught his arm. "Jack, I want you to know how much your friendship has meant to me. You've celebrated with me when I've celebrated, and you've encouraged me when I've questioned myself. I'm very lucky to have you. And you said something very wise that day at your house. About marriage and the hard work it takes. I wish I'd understood it like you did."

He was quiet a moment, staring out at the lake. "It's not going to work out between us, is it?"

I held his arm. An ache stabbed at my chest. A few months ago—maybe even a week ago—I would have questioned its meaning. I would have wondered if my feelings for Jack were true love. Now I understood them better. "I'm afraid not." I took a deep breath. "It would be selfish, I suppose, to want to hold on to our friendship in spite of everything."

Jack continued to stare out at the lake. I followed his gaze to the horizon, where the last glorious rays of the sun danced across the waves before it surrendered its post for the evening. Pink, orange, and yellow light scattered across the water like so many jewels cast away. Another perfect sunset.

"I don't know about that. We were great friends all those years while Emma was alive. I think she'd be disappointed in me if I gave up our friendship over a bruised ego. And I've had enough of regret for a lifetime." He took my hand and held it.

I smiled. "Me too."

We stood there together watching the sun slowly sink beyond the horizon. "Maybe I'll take you up on that coffee after all," he said. "And if you have the time for it, I think you're due for a rematch at Scrabble."

I laughed and we went into the cottage together. "I haven't eaten dinner yet. Fettuccine Alfredo?"

"Perfect."

After Jack left, I retreated to the spare bedroom—the one Celia and Jeff slept in when they visited. The one where I'd been stacking boxes of belongings from the house in Point-du-Fleuve. I had plans to unpack them and find places to store their treasures whenever things slowed down at the shop. As we headed into the busy summer season, that day hadn't arrived yet.

I wove my way between them to the back of the room, where I'd put the first boxes when I'd come home from that first clean-up day with Celia and Hannah. I unstacked a couple of the boxes, pulled out the bottom one, and rummaged through it until I found the photograph of my parents. I dusted it off and set it on the bed. I would put it on the mantle where it belonged. I dug further until I found the photo of me and Alfie. I found myself smiling back at his smile. It had always been infectious. Alfie had a kind of joy of life that was hard to quench. My anger and constant suspicion had almost done it. I guess it was understandable why he left.

I looked closer at his eyes. At the way he looked at me.

So *that* was true love.

21

___

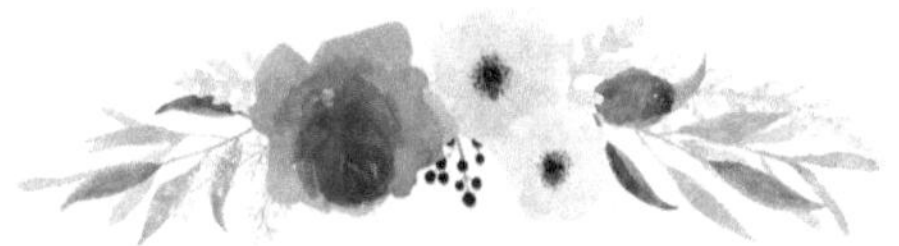

I woke up the next morning to the sound of the telephone ringing. I jumped out of bed, realizing I'd neglected to set my alarm the night before and I'd overslept.

"Hello?"

The line crackled. "Hi, Adele, it's me." Alfie's voice held that familiar warmth. "I had a crazy idea."

I laughed. "I might have one of my own. Why don't you go first?"

"I've been thinking a lot lately. About settling down. What would you think about my heading back your way?

My heart leapt. "I'd like that."

"Okay!" He chuckled. "That went well. Let me ask you this. How would you like to come down here first and travel with me one last time down Route 66? I figured maybe you'd like to bring your camera along. You could take some shots along the old Mother Road."

I'd never really traveled much at all. The idea sounded romantic. Spontaneous. I glanced at the calendar. "Alfie, I'd love to. But when? I'm just headed into the summer wedding season. And I've got classes booked. I couldn't leave for a couple of months. I'd have to talk to Jo-Ann—"

"Take your time. I'm not in any rush. You see if it'll work out and let me know."

"Okay, I will. But I've got to get ready for work now. I'm running late."

"All right. You call me when you have a chance."

"Okay. Bye now."

"Wait. What was your crazy idea?"

I laughed. "I was going to ask if you'd come up here and visit. But I like your idea better."

"Okay. We'll talk soon ... And Adele?"

"Yes?"

"I love you."

"I know."

22

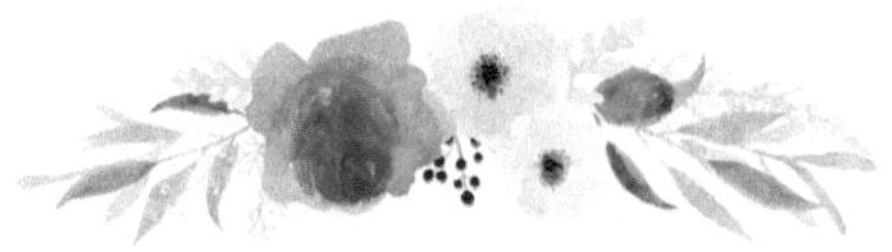

"**Y**ou sure you've got everything you need in that little backpack?" Jo-Ann fussed over me like a mother hen.

I adjusted the load on my back. "If you were carrying it, you wouldn't think it was so little. I'll be fine. And I have my cell phone in case you need to reach me."

She waved a hand at me. "Don't be silly. I know you hate that thing. We'll be just fine."

"And you're sure you're okay with your decision? You're not bound just because I've had this crazy idea, you know." Jo-Ann had told me she wasn't ready to go into retirement after all. She wanted to stay on with me at the shop and help out beyond the year we'd agreed on in the contract. And she'd stay and mind the shop while I was gone. Now that the summer weddings were behind us, we both agreed it was the best time for me to fly down and meet Alfie for our trip down Route 66.

We stood just outside airport security to say our final good-byes. "Are you nervous?"

I smiled. "Very. But excited too."

Jo-Ann hugged me. "I'll miss you, so I want to say 'hurry

back.' But I want you to have a good time and enjoy yourself." She shook a finger at me. "And don't do anything I wouldn't do."

I laughed. "I'll see you soon" I said and took my place in the line for security. A few moments later, I passed through the gate and lost sight of Jo-Ann.

My heart skipped a beat. Was I really doing this? What would it be like to see Alfie after all these years? He had sent me a recent photo in one of his letters, but it would still be strange to see him face-to-face. Thirty years had brought me gray hair and wrinkles. I still couldn't adjust to my own appearance in the mirror some days.

But one thing I knew I could count on. That look would be in his eyes.

VIP CLUB

Join my VIP Club to be the first to know about new releases and receive special bonuses available only to subscribers.

It's completely free to sign up to the VIP Club. You will never receive spam. You can opt out easily at any time.

Find the offer at careyjaneclark.com.

PLEASE LEAVE A REVIEW

If you have enjoyed this book, I would be very grateful if you could spend just five minutes leaving a review—as long or as short as you'd like. A review can be as simple as, "I enjoyed this book."

Reviews give other readers confidence in making informed choices about what they read.

Thank you very much.

ABOUT THE AUTHOR

Carey Jane Clark is the author of the Journeys of Hope series for adult readers and the Amazon Adventure middle grade series for children ages eight to twelve.

She actually answers emails from readers sent to carey@carey-janeclark.com.

Find her online: at careyjaneclark.com or connect on social media.

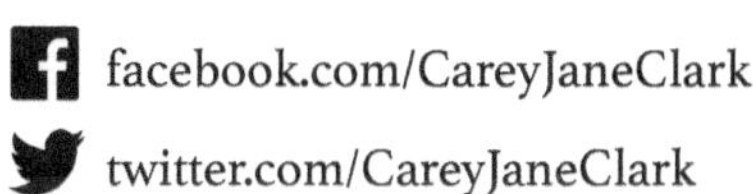

ALSO BY CAREY JANE CLARK

For adults:

After the Snow Falls

What the Girl Knew (Coming Soon)

For children 8-12:

Truth and the Tepawani

Trouble and the Tepawani (Coming Soon)

To be the first to be notified of new releases,

sign up for the VIP Club at

careyjaneclark.com

ACKNOWLEDGMENTS

I never thought I would write a book like *Love Me Forever*. Special thanks to author Alana Terry for planting the idea. And to my fellow Word Weavers, Eva Marie Everson, Cynthia Howerter, Susan Simpson, Penny Hunt, and Kim Miller for their critique and encouragement.

I also owe a debt of thanks to a special reader, Richard Owen, who let me know that there were readers out there who loved Alfie as much as I did. It was that gentle nudge that encouraged me to dig more into Alfie's story than appeared on the pages of *After the Snow Falls*.

Finally, I need to thank my family for their encouragement, for being my first readers, and for supporting my dream to see this story in print. I thank God for giving you to me.

www.ingramcontent.com/pod-product-compliance
Lightning Source LLC
Chambersburg PA
CBHW021703110726
47902CB00007B/2042